WORMWOOD

Wormwood

Mesmeris book three

K E Coles

Copyright KE COLES © 2016
KE COLES asserts the moral right to be identified as the author of this work. All rights reserved. If you have purchased the ebook edition please be aware that it is licensed for your personal enjoyment only and refrain from copying it.
Cover design Jennie Rawlings/Serifim.com. © 2016
Illustration by Ally Coles © 2015

Dedication

For my family.
Thank you for your invaluable feedback, advice, unwavering support, enthusiasm, and most of all for encouraging me whenever I feel I've lost the plot. You are all fantastic!
Also thank you to my fabulous beta readers , super talented writers, Gail Rennie and Ian Patrick

1. PAPA

Mother said he was evil, possessed by the devil. Perhaps she was right.

The first time she said it, Howard Pitt had been very small, six or seven years old, and he'd cried. It shamed him to remember it but he'd cried like a baby. He was never sure what sin he'd committed. When he asked, he was told he 'knew very well' before the wooden spoon whacked across his backside. Sometimes, when she was in a particularly bad mood, when someone or something had upset her, she used it on his shins, or his wrists, where the flesh was thin. On occasion she used the rolling pin. Sometimes Howard passed out. He would wake up in his bed with his mother stroking his forehead.

'Why do you have to make me angry?' she'd say, and he couldn't answer because he didn't know.

He tried to be good. He said his prayers every night, even made a small shrine in the corner of his tiny, damp box room. Every evening, he read a passage from the bible to his parents and yet still the sin came.

When he was eleven, it came in his dreams.

'Disgusting creature,' his mother called him as she whacked his bare behind with the wooden spoon. 'Spawn of Satan. Filthy child.'

He learned to love the bruises, to admire the colours, the depth, the changing quality. Every Sunday his parents took him to church, all dressed up in his grey three-piece old man's suit, his dark hair slicked over Hitler-style.

Howard didn't go to school. By shielding him from the

sinful behaviour of his peers, Mother ensured he only learned what was important – the Bible. The only book, she said, he would ever need.

They sent him to confirmation classes. The priest ruffled his hair. 'We're going to get along just fine, aren't we Howie?'

Howie? Howie?

'Yes,' Howard said, and they did.

Luckily, or unluckily for Howard, he wasn't one of *those* priests. If he had have been, he'd have seen the bruises and maybe done something to stop it. No, he was an upstanding, holy man full of God's love and forgiveness.

Howard detested him.

That's how he knew his mother was right. That's when his shrine became a different shrine, no longer to an ineffectual god, an insipid, pale lady in blue and a baby, but to something older, more powerful.

The cat was his friend. She understood him, knew his every thought. The cat brought gifts – mice, voles, baby birds. Together, they would lay them on the altar and Howard would recite runes and spells. Together, they planned their revenge.

Howard's shrine grew too elaborate for his small bedroom, so he and the cat transferred it to the cellar, somewhere Mother would never go, afraid of the spiders, afraid of the dark. Left undisturbed, Howard grew braver. He set up traps in the undergrowth of the garden, caught a rat, several stupid mice and one day, a squirrel.

Each creature was tied to the altar and ritually sacrificed. As the blood spilled, so Howard felt the strength flow into his being, the power of evil. The cat watched, unblinking, as Howard slit the rat's throat. The blood gurgled and spurted and Howard felt movement in his loins – power, excitement, lust.

The squirrel required heavy gloves. It fought like a demon, biting and scratching. Howard respected the creature so made it quick – a single slice across the throat. Other creatures, less noble ones, he tortured. Once he'd finished with them, he threw the remains to the cat. With each kill, Howard felt his strength growing.

Finally, on his fourteenth birthday, he felt strong enough to test his powers.

Mother was standing at the kitchen sink, arranging flowers in a vase. White flowers, for purity. Howard leaned against the doorjamb and watched her. The cat came and brushed against his leg. He leaned down and whispered in its ear. 'Now.'

Howard's heart raced as he watched the cat saunter across the room. Excitement made him breathless. Would it work? The spells, the sacrifices, would they all bear fruit?

The cat launched itself at Mother's leg, dug its claws into the flesh. Mother screamed and kicked her leg as though doing a jig. Howard laughed as the cat clung on, digging its claws deeper as trails of dark red, beautiful blood ran down Mother's legs.

'Arthuuuuur!' Mother punched the cat's head.

Its talons tore at her flesh. Rivulets of blood poured down, spattered on the floor.

'Do something,' Mother screamed at Howard.

While Howard thought about what that 'something' might be, the cat let go of its own volition. It wandered to the doorway and sat, lazily lifting one paw and cleaning it.

'You . . .'

Thwack, right across the head. Howard's ears rang. Stabbing pain shot from his neck to the top of his head. He crouched in the doorway, covering his head with his arms. Not that he was scared of her, not any more. He did it to hide his smile.

The cat winked at him.

'Rolling pin,' Mother screeched, looming over him. 'Rolling pin.'

Father scuttled into the kitchen, head bowed as though expecting the rolling pin himself. He opened the kitchen drawer.

'Legs and buttocks,' Mother said, 'and then kill the cat.'

'The cat?' Father and Howard said it at exactly the same time.

Mother turned scarlet. 'It's not a cat, is it?' she hissed through gritted teeth. 'It's his familiar.'

Father stared.

Howard stared. She knew. How did she know?

'Martha,' Father said. 'Are you sure? I mean . . .'

Mother clenched her fists and growled. 'Didn't I tell you? Didn't I? The boy's evil. He's brought evil into our home.'

Father looked from Mother to Howard and back, doubt written all over his face.

'Look at my leg,' Mother shrieked, pointing at the red, swollen, bloody mess. 'I saw him say something to the cat.' She pointed a shaking finger at Howard. 'Now, are you going to do it, Arthur, or do I have to?'

Father weighed the rolling pin in his hands. 'Cat first?' he said. 'Or . . .'

Mother looked around. They all followed her gaze.

Howard smiled. No cat anywhere.

The joy of having such power helped Howard with the pain. Father didn't relish punishing him, he knew, not like Mother did. Father hit him and apologised as he did it.

'She'll need to see bruises, you see,' he said as he hit Howard's shin.

Howard's vision blurred for a moment at the intense pain, then the ache dulled, warmed and became almost pleasurable. At least father hit his buttocks through his trousers, unlike Mother, who always insisted on removing his lower garments completely, muttering her disgust at what she called 'Satan's tool' before bending Howard over a stool and beating the life out of him.

'Don't touch the cat,' Howard said, once the thrashing was over.

'What?' Mother had been watching from the doorway. 'What do you mean, you stupid boy? It has to die.'

Howard looked into his mother's eyes. 'If you touch that cat, something bad will happen to you. Worse than that leg – far worse.'

Mother's eyes widened.

Father frowned. 'What does he mean, Martha?'

That was the first time Howard saw it – fear – fear that he had created. His mother was afraid of him.

The exhilaration, the joy instilled by that look in her eyes lasted for days. The beatings stopped. Howard missed them, missed the bruises, so much so that he would hit his own shins just to see the colours.

After the cat incident, things changed. Mother no longer looked Howard in the eye. She outlived her usefulness a few years later, so Howard took up an interest in cooking.

He created a casserole just for her. Accidental poisoning, the inquest found. Tragically, it seemed she'd mistaken hemlock for parsley, yew for rosemary. The sprinkling of wormwood dealt the final blow. Howard stifled his laugh as the coroner spoke, but perhaps Father noticed, because he became a nuisance from then on, watching every move with wary, suspicious eyes. He should never have threatened to call the police. That was stupid in the extreme. He'd left Howard no choice – no choice at all.

Howard wore the white, inverted cross he'd crafted from his father's bleached finger bones from that day onwards. It reminded him of that first ecstatic human sacrifice. The bone cross held untold power – the power of Mesmeris.

Alone in the family home, Howard worked and studied. He took a degree in law, then a master's. By the time he was twenty-one, he was Doctor Howard Pitt, already wealthy, already respected, already feared – except by the girls who lived opposite. Two sisters, they thought they were beautiful, desirable. They'd laughed at him all his life, whispered with their friends, their boyfriends, covering their mouths with their hands. They mocked him, brazen, taunting, unaware of his power.

They'd find out. Howard was just biding his time.

The eldest girl got pregnant. He knew it would happen, the way she flaunted herself. He watched her belly grow, watched her baby grow into a toddler. She called him Andreas. What kind of name was that for a boy? Art would be better – something short and snappy. What kind of life would a child have with a flighty girl like that? Children needed discipline, and Howard would be the one to provide it. Howard would be his Papa.

He followed them everywhere – the mother and child – for months, for years. *Three* years to be precise. He followed them to the shops, to the cinema.

And then, when he was ready, he followed them to the beach.

2. PEARL TWENTY YEARS LATER

The fifth of November. Bonfire night. Guy Fawkes.

Torches flamed around us as the skeleton danced before me, his black eyes staring into my soul. His head, the skull, stayed perfectly still as his body writhed and jerked to the pounding drumbeat. It reminded me of a hawk – the way his head didn't move. He stared into my eyes and I knew.

They were back.

I looked around for Spicer, to see if he'd felt it too, the recognition, but he was crouched down next to Lucas, buttoning up his coat.

The procession moved on down the narrow street, cheered by the villagers lining the pavements. The faces around me were smiling, laughing, happy. Families, children, the elderly. The whole village was there, enjoying the spectacle. Could it really be Mesmeris, or was it my over-active imagination at work again? Surely those taking part were locals. I was being ridiculous. There was nothing to be afraid of.

Smoke filled the air. I'd watched the students from the local college making the torches, dipping hessian fabric into black pitch and twisting it around the ends of a hundred wooden poles. I'd thought it exciting – a bit of fun. Now, though, held aloft by the bystanders, burning fiercely, they seemed to have hidden meaning, something insidious and evil. A troupe of dancing girls followed the drummers, their short skirts twirling in the flickering light. Schoolgirls. I knew some of them by sight. Nice girls from good families. This was nothing but a country celebration, nothing sinister at all. They wore sprigs of green in their hair. 'Wards off evil,' the woman next to me said, nodding, her glasses flashing as her head bobbed up and down. Well, that's all right then, I thought. All I had to do was stick a bit of green in my hair and bingo – no more evil Mesmeris, no more evil Papa. Sorted.

Lucas sat on Spicer's broad shoulders, his eyes alight, his mouth fixed in a beaming smile. He clapped his little chubby hands together over Spicer's blond head.

More drums approached, their beat slower this time, deeper. The drummers, all dressed in black, passed with their heads bowed. Their mournful beat, like the tolling of a bell, silenced the crowd. Behind them, someone dressed as a priest made the sign of the cross in the air as he walked, murmuring unintelligible words. The cross he drew was all wrong. The horizontal line was too low – too low. The cross was upside down. A shiver ran over my body.

'You okay?' Spicer said.

I nodded. 'Cold.'

He put an arm around my shoulder and pulled me close.

The fake priest passed by. Behind him, six black-clad men, faces covered with grinning clown masks, carried a wicker cage. Inside the cage crouched a figure made from straw, woven into the shape of a man.

Lucas tugged at Spicer's hair. 'Why's the man in the cage?' he shouted.

Spicer didn't hear him, so I relayed the question, shouting it into Spicer's ear.

'Guy Fawkes,' Spicer shouted. 'He's not real.'

Lucas frowned and pointed. 'Look.'

It did look uncannily lifelike in silhouette. Whoever the weaver was, they'd done a great job. It disappeared around the bend in the road and we were carried along by the villagers after the procession. Up the hill we went and into the field behind the church. By the time we got there, the wicker basket was balanced on top of the huge pile of wood in the middle of the field and the drummers were quiet.

The smell of burgers and hot dogs competed with that of burning tar. The sweet aroma of fried onions made us all hungry. I bought two coffees from the van – one for me, one for Spicer – and a veggie sausage in a bun for Lucas. My earlier fears seemed ridiculous now I was caught up in the festive atmosphere.

A rope barrier was set up around the bonfire. Behind it, crouched dark figures with what I assumed were going to be fireworks.

Lucas had never seen fireworks before but now he was almost three, Spicer said he was surely old enough to visit an organised display. The bangs always frightened me but the last thing I wanted was to make Lucas afraid too. The air was icy cold. The torches provided light but no heat, so that we grew impatient for the bonfire to be lit. It was already long past Lucas's bedtime and yet he didn't seem at all tired. With ketchup smeared all around his mouth, he looked so happy, bouncing there on Spicer's shoulders. He'd been right, of course, Spicer. It was no good wrapping Lucas up in cotton wool, making him fearful of anything and everything.

'That's no life,' Spicer had said, and I'd agreed. After all, I knew better than most. I spent my life being afraid.

The dancing girls had gone. I looked around, but could see no familiar faces, just lowered heads, or masks. Even the hotdog vans had turned off their lights. Stillness filled the air, as the crowd's expectation grew like a living thing.

Softly at first, the drums beat out a slow rhythm. The beats grew louder, faster. My heartbeat matched them. My mouth dried as dark figures held flaming torches to the base of the bonfire. At first, it looked as if they hadn't caught. Then it began spitting and crackling. Flames licked the lower branches as smoke billowed up, veiling the cage. The crowd roared its appreciation. People clapped and cheered.

The smoke cleared for a moment, blown by the wind, and the figure in the cage moved. For an instant, I thought I saw a face, desperate, pleading. Smoke veiled it again, as screams filled the air. No one seemed to hear them. Lucas wailed. Spicer lifted him from his shoulders and handed him to me. I cuddled his sobbing body in my arms as deafening explosions tore the air around us. Lucas went rigid.

'It's all right,' I shouted, but I doubt he heard me. I pushed my way through the crowd, with their beery breath and greasy chins. Through the noise and hiss and bangs of the fireworks, the crackling of the wood, the laughter, the shouting. On we went, down the hill and through the village.

And the harrowing screams followed us, all the way home.

3. PEARL

I plonked Lucas down in the hallway and turned on all the lights. The house was warm and bright and normal but Lucas's face looked ashen, his eyes huge and dark.

'It *was* a man,' he said quietly. He turned his back and went to sit on the sofa. He sat with his knees close to his chest and stuck his thumb in his mouth. All my practised, comforting words stayed unsaid. The way he'd said it – 'It was a man' – reminded me of his father. It was a fact as far as he was concerned and nothing I could possibly say would change his mind.

I jumped at the knock on the door.

Spicer's six-foot-something frame filled the doorway. 'What's up?' He looked past me, to Lucas. 'You okay, little man?'

'The fireworks.' I stood back and let him inside. 'They frightened him.'

Lucas shot me such a look. That a three year old was capable of such disdain was unbelievable. He took his thumb out. 'It was a man.' His mouth shut tight.

Spicer met my gaze. 'It's pretend,' he said. 'The man was made from straw.'

Lucas stared at him.

'It's all a game,' Spicer said. 'No one gets hurt.'

A flicker of doubt showed in Lucas's eyes.

Spicer sat next to him. 'It was a show, like on TV. D'you understand?'

'Promise?'

'Yes.' Spicer nodded. 'I promise there was no man.'

Lucas smiled.

'Happy now?'

He nodded. 'Will you be my daddy?'

My heart contracted. I stood in the open doorway. 'Who needs a daddy when you have a Spicer?' I said. 'No one else has a Spicer, only you. That means you're special.'

'But a daddy's there all the time,' Lucas said. 'Ben's daddy baths him *and* reads him stories.'

Spicer smiled. 'Well, how about I do that then?' He glanced at me. 'That okay?'

'Of course,' I said. No one would have made a better father than Spicer. Life would have been so much easier if we could have fallen in love, been a couple, but we weren't like that. We were best friends, with shared secrets, shared memories.

While Spicer bathed Lucas and put him to bed, I sat downstairs and drank a glass of red wine. It didn't have its usual relaxing effect. Instead it made my head muzzy and tired. Laughter filtered from upstairs, then Spicer's soft voice reading Lucas's current favourite, Paddington Bear. His voice grew gradually quieter, then silence. The stairs creaked as he crept downstairs. These small houses weren't built for big, sporty men like him. They were meant for small people like me. I poured him a glass and nodded towards the kitchen. The open plan house meant sound travelled upstairs. Lucas may have been asleep but I didn't want to risk it.

Spicer had to bend his head to go through the archway into the hall. Not that you could really call it a hall. Two steps and you'd walked it. I don't know what you would call it though – a space, perhaps. A connecting 'bit' between the front door, kitchen and living room.

'Why did you lie to him?' I said, once we were both sitting in the kitchen. The table and two chairs I'd squeezed into the corner looked like toys. I hadn't noticed how small everything was before. Now it felt like a dolls' house.

Spicer took a swig of the wine. 'Good stuff.'

'You lied, didn't you?'

'No.' He avoided my gaze, a sure sign I was right.

'There *was* a man. He was real.'

Spicer's mouth shut tight, but he didn't deny it.

'Wasn't he?' I could feel the panic rising, bubbling, but I couldn't stop it.

He sighed and closed his eyes. 'No Pearl, it was straw.' His eyes opened, and I saw pity in them, pity and exasperation.

'The skeleton . . .'

He rolled his eyes. 'What about it?'

'It was Leo.' As soon as I said it, I knew I should have kept my mouth shut.

Spicer groaned. 'For f . . . ' He lowered his voice, leaned across the table. 'He's *dead*, remember? You *killed* him, for Christ's sake.'

His words landed like a punch, knocked me back in my seat.

And there was Leo, in front of me, at *that* moment, the moment he realised I wasn't going to reach for him. The moment he knew nothing would stop him falling backwards, down, down into the oily black water. The panic in his eyes, the disbelief, the horror. How had I forgotten that? A shiver ran over me, from head to toe. I couldn't look at Spicer, couldn't speak, couldn't think. So I stood instead, and went to the sink. I threw dirty dishes into the empty bowl. Crash, crash they went, one on top of the other, each louder than the last, until a dark glass bowl, Lucas's favourite, shattered. I thought it was Pyrex, unbreakable, but I was wrong. Shards of it flew everywhere. An explosion of glass. Tiny slivers rained down onto the draining board, the work surface, my head, my hands, the floor. I waited for the sound of tinkling glass to stop.

I stared at the wall and wished Spicer would go, just go and leave me. Of course he didn't, but fussed about instead, telling me to stand still, finding the dustpan and brush and sweeping it up. I couldn't look at him.

I heard the bin open, heard the glass shards hit the plastic, heard the brush sweeping the pan clean.

'Come here.' His hands touched my shoulders.

'Get off me.'

'Fine.' And I thought, he'll leave it now. He'll go and I can get my head together, but no. There he was standing with his hands in the air, which you'd think meant surrender, except he was opening his mouth and he was going to speak and I couldn't. I couldn't.

I lifted my hand so it blocked out his face. 'I don't want to talk about it.'

'Pearl, you need . . .'

'I *said* . . .' Damn it! Why did my voice have to wobble like that? I needed him out of there so I could cry, or think, or whatever. 'Not now. Please.'

'Right.' He picked up his bag, swung it over his shoulder. He looked suddenly weary as he stepped into the hallway. I followed him. I'd wanted him to leave but now I was afraid. Without him the house would feel empty. Without him, my thoughts would run free, lead me God knows where.

His hand was on the latch, pulling it down.

'So they're not back?' I said.

He didn't turn around but I could see he'd had enough, by the stiff shoulders, the ramrod straight back. 'No.' The word was clipped, terse.

'No,' I said, as if repeating it would make it true, but he was already out of there anyway, striding out to his car, rigid with anger.

I locked and bolted the door behind him.

They weren't back. I was being an idiot. The wicker man was straw, and everything was right with the world.

Definitely.

4. ART

The rusted shackle bit into the raw skin around his ankle. He shifted position. Pain shot up his leg, made his eyes water. He turned his back to the driving rain. It made little difference. His clothes were soaked through, his dark hair plastered to his head.

It was the rain that kept him alive. Without it, he'd have already died. He tried to stop himself tilting his head back, opening his mouth. Better to get it over with. It was impossible. His body's need for fluid overpowered logic. It amazed him, the survival instinct.

Raindrops bounced on the concrete of the courtyard, bounced on his head, on the freezing, skeletal hand that clung to the tree trunk. His fingers had long since grown numb, but he clung on as if his life depended on it, which it did, or at least his eyesight.

Even the ravens had taken cover, stopped circling him. They waited under their shelters. He could see their eyes glittering. Watching, waiting for him to fall, to lose consciousness. At one time, he thought they waited for death. Now he knew better. They'd go for the eyeballs first.

He leaned his head against the rough bark of the spindly tree and closed his eyes. Immediately, he began to dream. He forced himself awake. That way lay death. That way lay disaster.

The ravens weren't the only ones watching him. He could feel Papa's calculating gaze. Would he let him die? Perhaps, but there was no thrill in that. Surely, if Papa wanted him dead, he'd have sacrificed him days ago, weeks maybe, while he still had some fight left. After all, it was the struggle that was the turn-on – the fight for life. No struggle, no rush.

He always knew when Papa was there, behind the reflective glass window – a sixth sense, an instinct. Perhaps others were there too. Perhaps they were laughing – or excited, buzzing. Waiting for the end, hoping he'd give them a spectacle. He'd done it himself. He knew the way it worked.

A gust of wind whirled around inside the courtyard. How wind got in there when it was surrounded by three-storey blocks, he'd never quite worked out. So cold. So cold. His feet were as numb as his hands. He'd lost count of how long he'd been shackled there. Days and nights anyway.

At least the rain washed away some of the stench of his own waste, of the blood from the latest sacrifice. A measly cat hung from the branch above him. As it rotted, it seeped foul-smelling fluid. Funny how the ravens didn't touch it. Everything else that had hung from that tree had been stripped of its flesh within a week.

Sometimes he thought he saw what Papa called his mementos – skeletons of past sacrifices – birds, animals, humans, hanging white and glowing in the darkness. When he blinked, sometimes they vanished, sometimes not. Sometimes they moved closer while he wasn't looking, the bastards. If he'd believed in ghosts . . . Well, he didn't. God knows, if they existed, they'd have come for him long ago. None of the deaths bothered him. They'd never haunted his dreams. The pleading, the fear, the desperation didn't touch him. The only emotion he'd ever felt was distaste – mild or intense, depending how pathetic they were.

The raindrops stung on the ends of his fingers where his nails had once been. Not so numb then. Not yet.

At least he was outside, not down in the dungeon. That had been the worst. That had been when he still cared. Now, he'd accepted his fate, whatever that would be. All he had to do was endure, and wait for Papa to decide – endure and hope the ravens didn't get his eyes.

5. PEARL

Rain pulsed down, eased off then intensified, slamming into the glass.

'Mummy?'

'Mmm?' I wondered where Art was, whether he too was watching the rain. I wondered if he ever thought of me, or his child, our little Lucas standing behind me, tugging at my sleeve. No doubt he'd forgotten us, caught up in some scheme, ruining someone's life – or ending it. I shivered.

'Mummy.'

Everyone said Art was evil. Evil. So that was that then. I'd moved on anyway. A mistake, that's all it had been. But when I looked at my boy, I didn't see a mistake. He looked just like his father – same intense blue eyes, same soft, sculpted lips. But Lucas wasn't evil. Lucas was good. He filled my life with joy, with light. So out of evil came good, and I regretted none of it, except that I wished Art were different.

Lucas climbed onto my lap, put his hands either side of my face and turned it, forcing me to look at him. 'Why are you crying?'

'I'm not.'

'You are.' He wiped a finger across my cheek and showed me the wetness.

'Sometimes people cry when they're happy.' I smiled to prove it. 'I was just thinking how lucky I am to be your mummy.'

'You're not sad?'

'Of course not,' I said.

'Good.' He hugged me, his arms tight around my neck. As he grew heavy and his breathing regular, I realised he'd fallen asleep. I felt such a powerful wave of love for him, it almost hurt. How idiotic to be sad when I had the most wonderful child. Art was in the past. It was stupid to let myself think of him – stupid and pointless.

I'd believed he was good underneath it all, under the hard shell, the indifference, the coldness. I believed it because I wanted it to be true. I wanted him to be Jack I suppose, but he wasn't. He would never be.

It didn't stop me thinking of him every day, several times a day. Not that I'd admit it. I'd done so once, to my counsellor, and that had been a mistake. A fixation, she called it. She pointed out that our relationship had consisted of precisely five shags over a matter of weeks. She suggested that the 'relationship' part of it was my 'construction' – in other words, in my head. He, she surmised, was just a 'lad getting his leg over'. She didn't know Art of course. 'Lad' was hardly a term I'd have used. He was the least laddish person I knew. *I* was more of a lad than he was.

So I kept it to myself, my longing for him, my longing to be desired. It felt shameful, wanting to be looked at 'like that'.

Not that he'd ever desired me, not really. Not him. Not Jack. Not anyone. They'd only seduced me because they'd been told to, ordered to.

Was I that ugly? That hideous that no one would ever want me? Maybe. Physically, I was ordinary. A bit pale, pasty, my breasts too small, my legs too short, bum too big. A pear, in effect. My face was a face. Nothing remarkable

– two eyes, a nose, a mouth – the usual. What was it then that made me so repulsive? Need. That's what it was. And loneliness. People sensed that. It must have come off me in waves. People sensed it and they moved away. It made them uncomfortable. I frightened them with my hunger.

So I never mentioned Art, never talked about him except sometimes to strangers. 'My boyfriend's away,' I'd say. Ha! Yes, he was 'away' but he wasn't, had never been, my boyfriend.

Anyway . . .

We had new lives now, me and my boy. Lucas. The future could be anything we wanted it to be. If only I could stop dwelling on the past

The moon broke through the clouds and I thought maybe it was a sign that this time, *this* time, things would work out.

We'd moved to the village to get away from Mesmeris. Stuck in the middle of nowhere, it seemed to have been lost in time. Mum and Dad had bought a small house as a retirement home. They swore they were going to buy one anyway, before they found out about Lucas. I suppose they didn't want me to feel guilty. 'You'll be safer there,' Dad had said. 'A new estate always has lots of families. It'll be perfect for Lucas.'

And it *was* perfect for us, but I found it hard to believe they'd want to retire to a new-build starter home. I didn't argue. Keeping Lucas away from Mesmeris was the main thing. I found a job I could do from home – data input. It wasn't glamorous but it just about paid the bills and meant I didn't have to farm Lucas out to someone else. Spicer moved nearby, even though I told him I would be fine. He said he wanted a new start too. He rented a bedsit on the outskirts of the local town, about five miles away. He said he liked it there, liked being respectable, being a proper copper with no hiding, no skulking, no pretending to be who he wasn't. Of course, he *was* still pretending. His name wasn't really Spicer but Marcus, and everyone thought he was Lucas's father, when he wasn't. That's what Mesmeris did – to those who survived it. It changed their lives, made them different people, turned them into frightened, nervy, suspicious liars.

A road ran through the centre of the village where Lucas and I lived. Traffic hurtled past, en route between one town and another, barely noticing the scattered, unremarkable council-built houses strung along it. It wasn't a pretty village. More functional, but the village green hosted cricket matches in the summer and the whole village turned out to watch.

Not long after we moved there, when Lucas was still a toddler, I'd taken him to watch the blacksmith shoe a horse. It was autumn, the air heady with the smell of new-mown hay. There was something melancholy about the afternoon – the sunshine, the sweet air, the buzzing insects. It was all too beautiful, too perfect to last.

The stone-built smithy was on the coast road. The blacksmith had coppery, curly hair and muscles – lots of muscles. Sweat shone on his arms as he held the iron shoe in the blazing furnace until it was white hot. He lifted it onto the anvil and hammered at it. Sparks flew as it changed from white to yellow to orange, to red. Lucas gasped and clapped. He got a smile from the blacksmith for that. I wondered if I'd be happy married to a farmer, or a blacksmith, or anyone safe and wholesome, any decent, working man. I wondered if anyone like that would want a crazy head case like me as a wife. I decided not, probably.

Afterwards, we walked through narrow lanes lined with tall hedges, over a stile and down a meandering path to a small, pebbly cove.

There were other beaches and we explored them all over the next few months. At first, I was afraid to go anywhere alone, but as the months passed and the seasons changed, I really began to believe they were finished – Mesmeris. I began to feel safe.

On Sundays I took Lucas to Dad's church and then went back to the Vicarage for Sunday lunch. Sometimes my younger sister Lydia would be there. Almost always Dad's curate, Andrew, joined us. He was pretty much part of the family. He and Dad no longer shut themselves in the study for hours on end, so I assumed they'd stopped fighting Mesmeris. They still had a thing about cults though.

'They're a little on the pagan side where you are, Pearl, aren't they?' Andrew said, pushing his glasses higher. They slipped down his nose immediately.

Dad chewed on his roast beef. It took some chewing, like eating cardboard.

'Oh, I don't know,' Mum said.

It had been my turn to cook, so I'd chosen a joint of topside. It had looked so good in the supermarket. Half price too. Bargain, I'd thought.

'They stick heather in their hair,' Lydia said, eyes wide.

'Rowan,' Dad said.

'Well rowan then.' Lydia rolled her eyes. 'Same difference.'

Andrew nodded. 'Half of them don't go to church but organise a bonfire and they're *all* out.' He waved his hands in the air. Lucas liked it and copied him, giggling.

'It's village life, Andrew,' Dad said.

'Hmm . . .' A bald spot was appearing on Andrew's head. It made me sad, as if his life was slipping away from him. Of course it was slipping away from all of us really, but he was the only balding one. I wished he had someone – a girlfriend maybe.

'Odd about the disappearances though, don't you think?' he said. 'You'd expect one or two I suppose, but *three?*'

Dad shrugged. 'Teenagers run away, especially in the country. I mean, what *is* there for them there?' He waved an arm in a general southerly direction.

'Bugger all,' Lydia said, under her breath.

'They want excitement,' Dad said. 'The big city.'

Lydia snorted. 'I think it's *them.*'

All eyes turned my way.

I concentrated on trying to cut through a roast potato.

'Nonsense,' Dad said.

'That's all behind us,' Mum said, in her sensible, nurse's voice.

'Yes,' Dad and Andrew said together. A chorus of priests.

What an embarrassment I was for my poor parents. Vicars weren't meant to have single mothers for daughters, grandchildren fathered by criminals, murderers, psychos. I tried to make it up to them, tried to be the daughter they'd hoped for – someone kind, patient, chaste and good – and it exhausted me. My nature wasn't good, but I was working on it. They deserved better, so I studied, and worked hard. I helped out in church, in Sunday school. I didn't go out, didn't get drunk, didn't smoke or take drugs, didn't flirt or have lovers. I did nothing but work to make them proud.

And every night I cried, every single night, for the life I'd thrown away.

In the mornings I'd tell myself I was a stupid cow. I was safe, wasn't I? I had a roof over my head, a job I could do from home, a car, enough food to eat, a loving family. I had Lucas. I had so much to be grateful for, and then I felt guilty for not being grateful.

Even Spicer had settled. He was playing rugby again. That, I suppose, gave him excitement. And the girls. He had lots of girls in his bed. It wasn't surprising. He was good-looking, hunky, gentle and tough at the same time. Everything a normal girl could want. Still, sometimes I thought he missed it all – the adrenaline, the danger. It was probably me doing that thing, projecting my own emotions onto him. I was always doing that, my counsellor told me. That's what I'd done with Art, she said. He had no emotions, she said.

How she could know that when she'd never met him, I don't know. When she'd never had his warm hands sliding over her body, never had his mouth on hers, never had him move inside her. She did though. She knew him for what he was. Everyone knew him for what he was, except me.

And there I was again, thinking about him, crying again, over him.

I needed to curb my recklessness, they said. Think of the consequences of my actions *before* doing anything. One can't be reckless when one has a child, they said, when one has responsibilities – as if I didn't know that, as if I was stupid.

So there was no recklessness any more, not from me. I buried myself in work, in church, in being a better person.

All I had to do was keep Lucas safe.

Easy.

6. SPICER

Spicer pulled on a t-shirt, sat on the edge of his bed and stared gloomily at his poky, shabby living space, at the scuffed and marked magnolia walls, the chipped paintwork. He kept meaning to look for somewhere better, somewhere with a separate bedroom and living area, but stuff always got in the way and besides, he was on his own. It hardly seemed worth the effort.

At least he was up before the alarm for once. Usually he had to drag himself into consciousness, longing to dive back under the covers and forget the world. The nightmares left him knackered most days. The load of paperwork waiting for him on his desk every morning didn't help matters. Dull stuff that a muppet could sort. The runaway kids case would have been interesting, but that was given to someone else. Spicer had mentioned Mesmeris, the way they targeted disaffected teenagers, but no one seemed interested. Two of them had turned up safely anyway. The other, Danny, was almost sixteen and had run away several times before. They went through the motions, putting photos up on the board etc, but Spicer didn't see anyone making any real effort to find him. 'He'll come back when he runs out of money,' they said, 'just like he always does.'

Spicer hoped they were right. Even if they weren't, it was unlikely they'd involve him in the investigation. After two and a half years, he was still 'the new boy'. Antisocial behaviour, shoplifting and car crime generally came his way. Not exactly the exciting life he'd imagined.

Not that morning though. That morning he was going to be driving north and sitting in on an interview with his old boss, DI Jim Macready. The fact that Jim was involved made him twitchy as well as excited. The last thing he wanted was to get involved with Mesmeris again. Even paperwork was better than that. Ever since the case against them had been thrown out by the CPS, he'd put them in a compartment in the back of his mind – a locked, bolted compartment – and that was where they were going to stay.

As he drove to Jim's station, he practised what to say if the DI mentioned the M word, how to tell him he wanted out. The guv had been like a father to him over the last few years. Not only had he wangled Spicer a place back on the force, but he knew him, the *real* him, his background, his family, all the trauma he'd been through. And he was always there, always supportive, in his gruff, foul-mouthed way. Even thinking about him made Spicer smile. He didn't want to let Jim down, but he had a new life now, a safe, pleasant, undemanding one.

All Jim had said was, 'I have something here that may interest you,' anyway. Perhaps it was nothing to do with *them*. He laughed at the thought. It was *always* something to do with them if Jim was involved. 'I'd like you to sit in on an interview,' he'd said. 'I've sorted it with your DCI.'

Sitting in on an interview. How dangerous could it be?

Jim was waiting for him in reception. The first thing Spicer noticed was the new shoes. Modern, trendy, the kind of thing a mid-life crisis bloke would wear. He'd shaved too. And had a haircut, no less.

'Looking smart there, sir.'

Jim raised his eyebrows but said nothing. He steered Spicer through the security door. His paunch had definitely shrunk. His shirt was crisply ironed – not the usual creased mess. Not only that, but he smelled of aftershave.

Spicer hid his smile. A woman. Had to be.

'Someone crawled in here this afternoon,' Jim said.

'*Crawled?*'

'On hands and knees.' Jim kept his voice low. 'Mentioned Mesmeris.'

'Ah!' Spicer looked back at the door. He should tell him now, walk away.

'Good to see you, lad.' Jim slapped him on the back. 'You'll be pleased to know I've had you seconded to my investigation. The old team back together, eh?'

Spicer forced a smile. Pleased wasn't quite how he felt, but his curiosity was piqued and he liked the boss, respected him more than any other copper he'd ever met. He'd just see what this was all about, then back out if necessary. Plenty of time to change his mind.

A uniformed constable stood outside the interview room. He nodded towards the door. 'Superficial wounds, sir. Medic says he's okay for interview.' He pushed the door open and stood aside.

The victim looked like any other drunk slumped over the table. A bit bloodied, but a punch up was hardly unusual any day of the week. His hair was dark and greasy. His hands filthy.

He sat up. Even in profile, there was no mistaking him.

Spicer turned his back and left the room. Outside, he leaned back against the wall, exhaled. That had been close

– too close.

The door opened and Jim came out. He shut the door behind him. 'So?' His hard eyes glittered. 'You know him?'

Spicer nodded. 'Foot soldier. Malki. He knows me – well.'

Jim whistled between his teeth. 'Did he clock you?'

'No.'

'Sure?'

'One hundred percent.'

'Good.' Jim slapped Spicer's arm, grinned. 'Hey, this could be our lucky day.'

Spicer wasn't so sure.

'Observation room for you, my lad.' Jim led him into the office next door where a woman sat watching Malki through the two-way mirror.

'It's okay, Sam,' Jim said. 'Spicer here's taking over.'

'Oh, right.' She flashed Spicer a fake smile. 'Of course. They're your mates, aren't they?'

Spicer kept his mouth firmly shut and moved aside to let her leave the room.

'You wouldn't be still working for them, would you?' she said as she passed, head tilted to one side.

'No.' If she thought he was going to rise to that, she was mistaken. So she didn't trust him. Maybe none of them did except Jim. He could live with that. No one hated Mesmeris more than he did – no one.

The door closed and Spicer sank gratefully into the chair, glad to be alone. Seeing Malki had shaken him up more than he'd realised. The last couple of years had muted his memories, made him wonder if Mesmeris were really such a threat. Malki brought the reality back – the horror and the evil.

Spicer turned his attention to the interview room.

Malki fidgeted on the green plastic chair. His eyes darted here and there. He clenched his hands, unclasped them, shifted in his seat. When the door opened, he visibly jumped.

Jim sat opposite him. 'Are you sure you don't want a lawyer?'

'Fuck no,' Malki said. 'Don't trust them wankers.'

Jim smirked.

A PC came in with two teas and placed them on the table. She then sat on the chair by the door.

Malki shook his head. 'I'm not – I'm not talking to no one but you, man.' He pointed at Jim.

Jim nodded at the PC. She got up and left the room, shutting it quietly behind her.

'So,' Jim placed his hands together, elbows on the table, 'Malki. What can we do for you?'

Malki stared. 'How d'you know my name?'

Spicer murmured, 'Nice one, guv.' A quiver of excitement ran through him. He'd forgotten the feeling – the rush of danger – forgotten how it made him feel alive. He hated it and yet loved it at the same time.

Jim frowned, pretended to check his notepad, leafed through a couple of pages. 'It *is* Malki, isn't it?'

'Yeah, but . . .' Malki shook his head. 'Listen. He's gonna kill me.'

'He?'

'Him. You know.' He twitched with irritation, leaned forward, lowered his voice. 'Art.'

'Art?' Jim made a good job of looking clueless.

'Fuck's sake.' Malki's hands waved about, jerkily. '*Him.*'

Jim slurped at his tea.

Malki leaned right across the table. 'You know him. He's an Elite, right? In Mesmeris?'

'Ah.' Jim slurped at his tea again. '*That* Art.' Everything about his body language said he was relaxed, enjoying himself. The polar opposite to Malki.

'You gonna put him away, right?'

'Why would I do that?'

'He's a head case.' Malki tapped his temple. 'He attacked me.' The tip of his tongue flicked across his lips as he spoke, like a snake tasting the air. 'I fought back, didn't I? Anyway,' He sat back, folded his arms across his chest, 'I tied him to a tree.'

'*You* tied Art to a tree?' Jim said.

'No chance,' Spicer muttered into the microphone. 'Not unless he had help.'

Jim smirked. 'And you did this on your own?'

Malki leaned forward, eyes narrowed, mouth twisted. 'Yeah. I could string you up too, no problem.'

Jim chuckled. 'Think I'll pass on that, thanks.'

Malki stared. 'You think you're safe cos you're a copper?' From pitiful wreck to full-blown evil in seconds.

'Careful, guv,' Spicer said. 'He's a coward, but he's quick, vicious.'

Jim glanced up at the two-way mirror and smiled.

You should be afraid, Jim, Spicer thought. He's not messing.

Malki sniffed, wiped his nose with the back of his hand. 'You better go and get him, I reckon. Been there a while. Could be dead by now.'

'Been where?'

Malki grinned, revealing a chipped front tooth. 'In the old place. Brighton.'

'Old place?'

'Moved out, yeah.'

Jim looked up at Spicer, frowned. This was news to them. Pitt's Brighton mansion had been the cult's headquarters for years and no one, not one of their snitches had mentioned a move.

Jim's relaxed posture didn't change. The only sign he was rocked by the revelation was the tightening of his grip around the pen, the whitening of his knuckles. 'So, where've they gone?'

Malki did a theatrical shrug. 'Search me.'

Jim scribbled something on his notepad, then sat back. 'I have to advise you that, even with your . . .' He waved a hand, 'obvious wounds, it's unlikely he'll go to prison.'

'What?' A drop of mucus hung from Malki's nose. '*What?*'

Jim shrugged. 'A first offence and if, as you say, he's been tied to a tree and left to die . . .' He sighed. 'Well, it could be you who ends up in court.'

'*Me?*' Malki's eyes bulged. 'What the . . ? What about the other stuff he done.'

'Stuff?' Jim said.

'Them murders.' Malki's face screwed up. 'It was *him*, wasn't it? Been doin' stuff off his own bat. Papa din't know nothing about it.'

'Shit.' Spicer's stomach clenched. Had Art been involved in his sister's murder after all? The thought brought him out in a cold sweat.

Malki patted his jacket. 'I got a disc here. It's all on it – all of it.' He chewed his thumbnail. His eyes flicked from Jim to the door and back, Jim to the door and back. 'I weren't there. Don't know nothing about it. None of us do. Was only him.'

'Who gave you the disc?'

Malki swallowed. 'Found it.'

'*Found* it?'

'Yeah. Yeah.' He wasn't even concentrating, seemed more interested in the door. The way he kept looking behind him, Spicer was surprised he didn't crick his neck.

Jim pursed his lips. 'And Art didn't – come across it when he assaulted you?'

'In my pocket, wan it?' Malki chewed his nails again.

Jim held out a hand, palm upwards. 'Let's have it then.'

'Nah, nah!' Malki wiped sweat from his forehead. 'First you gotta swear he'll go down, cos if he don't . . .'

'I can't lock him up if you don't give me the evidence,' Jim said. 'So hand it over.'

'You gotta keep me safe, man. It's your job.'

'If the evidence is conclusive, I'll . . .'

'No, no. Not good enough.' Malki leaned over the desk, licked his lips. 'See, if you don't lock him up, he'll find me. And when he finds me . . .' He lowered his eyes, bit his nails.

Jim stood and held out a hand. 'Nice to meet you, Malki.'

'Where you going?'

'We'll do our best to protect you, as we do for every law-abiding citizen, but . . .' He shrugged.

'Shit, man.' Malki's agitation was painful to watch. Not a single part of his body was still – everything twitching.

'Shit.' He shot a glance behind him at the door, then pulled a DVD from his inside pocket and handed it over.

Jim looked straight at Spicer with a small smile. He switched on the recorder, recited the date, time and persons present. 'Okay.' He sat back. 'Let's start at the beginning.'

7. PEARL

It was Spicer who'd talked me into applying for university. I thought he was joking at first. Me? Study for a degree?

'What in?' I said. 'I can't do anything. Well, nothing but make a mess of my life anyway.'

'Writing.'

I laughed. 'Don't be daft.'

'You're good. Those stories you write for Lucas – they're great.'

'They're silly.' And they were. Funny tales to make Lucas laugh, stories of accident-prone animals. Nothing that hadn't been done before – and much better – by somebody else.

'They're not. And what about the other stuff you wrote . . .'

'That's personal.' I stood, furious. I should never have shown him, never. I should never have written it in the first place. My counsellor's stupid suggestion. A way of dealing with 'trauma', she said. Writing it all down would be cathartic. I'd be able to offload all the fear and horror and move on.

I stood in front of the fireplace and tried to calm down. I'd only shown Spicer so he would understand – about Jack, about his murder. So he'd know why I sometimes threw a wobbly. He'd promised to forget it, swore he'd never mention it again. So much for *that*.

I watched him in the mirror, watched him close his eyes and pinch the top of his nose between thumb and forefinger. 'I just think it would be good for you, that's all,' he said.

He was my best friend. My very best friend.

'What about Lucas? What am I supposed to do with him? Leave him on his own all day?'

'Nursery,' he said, wearily. 'It's what normal people do, Pearl.'

Well that was that then. 'Normal' was hardly a word that applied to me.

He left shortly after that and we didn't speak of it again – the writing or the idea of university – but I kept thinking about it all the same, wondering if I was capable of the work and afraid to think I might be in case I failed. I applied to study part-time without telling Spicer I'd done it. That way I wouldn't have to tell him if they laughed in my face. I only applied to one uni – the local one that used to be a polytechnic or technical college or something similar. I tried not to let myself imagine, even for an instant, myself in a cap and gown, a graduate, a BA, because a painful quiver of excitement would shoot through me whenever I did. Hope and terror in equal measure.

I sent some samples of my writing, including the *one*, the so-called catharsis. After they'd disappeared into the ether, I did my best to forget about it, and failed miserably.

Less than a week later, they offered me an unconditional place.

I couldn't believe it. I read and re-read the email at least ten times. I was so excited I couldn't sit still. I told Spicer first, and he whooped down the phone. He sounded so pleased for me that I didn't stop smiling for hours. He ran security checks on all the local nurseries and picked out the safest. It seemed such a good idea in theory. On that first morning though I almost changed my mind. Lucas looked far too small to leave with strangers, with people he didn't know, people *I* didn't know. If Spicer hadn't been there, maybe I would have taken him home again. Failing, giving up before I'd started, felt safer, more comfortable. It was what I knew after all.

'It's not just you,' Spicer said. 'Think about Lucas. He needs time away from you so he can grow up, make friends.'

'But how do we know it's safe?'

'We've run all the checks, and more.' All the checks maybe, but his gaze still scanned the high railings around the outside playing area as though it was a military barracks, not a nursery school.

'You're not sure, are you?' I said.

'Of course I am.' He smiled. 'It'll be good for him – and you.'

Perhaps, I thought, but if he doesn't like it I'll never send him again. Of course he loved it, and I felt a tug of disappointment, as if I was suddenly redundant, as if I'd lost part of him already. He had to grow away from me, I knew that, and I had to let him go, but not yet.

Once my course started I felt better. My life became interesting and even sometimes fun. Using my brain made me happy. I made friends, but I was still glad Spicer was around. Whenever I panicked about Lucas, he would drop everything and come over. No one could calm me down like him, put things in perspective like him. I should have trusted him, but it was hard sometimes.

As I drove Lucas to nursery one morning, I spotted him coming out of the newsagents. Someone walked behind him, someone in a khaki Parka. I was so sure it was Leo. My pulse quickened. I felt sick. I couldn't get a good look at him, Spicer was blocking my view. Another car hooted and I realised I'd slowed to a crawl in the middle of the road, holding up the traffic. I held a hand up in apology and pulled in alongside the pavement.

'Stay there.' I opened my door, looked back at the shop. No sign of Spicer. No sign of a green Parka. 'Come on.' I lifted Lucas out of his seat, walked along the parade of shops, looking in each one, but they'd gone.

I called Spicer.

'I just saw you,' I said, 'at the shops.'

He'd popped in for a bottle of water. His voice sounded normal, not shifty, not as if he was hiding something, but you could never tell with Spicer. He was a good liar. He'd had to be, living with them, with Mesmeris.

'Did you see anyone you knew?' Even as I said it, I knew it sounded weird.

'*What?*' I could imagine his frown.

'I just . . . I just thought you were with someone.'

'Like who?' he said, and I could tell he'd guessed what I was thinking, because he sighed, loudly. 'No, I haven't seen Leo,' he said. 'In fact, I've never seen any ghost.'

I laughed, hoping it would stop him being annoyed. 'It was just someone in a Parka.' Tears pricked my eyes. 'Must go – nursery.'

'Are you okay?'

'Absolutely. See you soon.' I ended the call, annoyed with myself for phoning him. Of course it hadn't been

Leo. Spicer would have noticed him.

No, Leo was dead, *that* was why it wouldn't be him. I really needed to remember that.

8. PEARL

A travelling fairground came to the local town. We went one afternoon – Lucas, Spicer and I. It was a perfect end to the day – the rides golden in the last faint rays of sunshine, seagulls keening overhead. Spicer was happier than I'd ever seen him. We watched Lucas go round and round in a chariot, squealing with delight every time he saw us, while we waved and laughed. Spicer had a go at the shooting range. Every single shot was on target.

'Bit of a marksman, your man,' the stallholder said.

I didn't bother to explain that he wasn't 'my man', or indeed that he was a police-trained firearms officer. It was none of his business.

Spicer held Lucas up to choose a prize. He picked out a huge white teddy bear, the biggest one there. The stallholder handed it to him. It was almost as tall as he was.

'Thank you,' Lucas said.

Spicer lowered him to his feet and ruffled his hair. 'What are you going to call him?'

'Frank,' Lucas said, with a small frown. Then, 'Incense.'

Spicer raised his eyebrows in mock horror. 'You spend *far* too much time in church, young man.'

I laughed. 'We're so lucky to have you, Spicer.'

'I'm the lucky one.' He bent his head and kissed me. On the lips. Just a light touch and gone.

I jumped. It sent such a jolt through me.

'Sorry.' His eyes darkened.

'No, I . . .' I didn't know what I felt – shocked, yes, horrified even. 'I was just surprised.'

'Me too. I was aiming for your cheek.' He laughed, and it was all right again. Everything was normal.

But I kept thinking how Spicer's aim was always spot on and wondering what it meant, if anything. It didn't fit with our relationship and yet it had felt so good because it had been forever since anyone had touched my mouth with theirs. I could still feel his lips on mine, and when we spoke, whenever I looked at him, I found myself looking at it, his mouth, at the soft, pale pink lips, and thinking about it, and wishing he'd do it again, and at the same time praying he wouldn't, ever.

What felt like a huge thing to me evidently didn't to Spicer. I doubt he even thought of it again. For him, it was one of many, meant nothing. He'd probably been on auto-pilot, had mistaken me for one of his women, just for an instant.

I dreamed about it for weeks, but the kisser was never Spicer. Sometimes it was Art, so that I woke longing for him with an intensity I thought might kill me. At other times it was someone I'd seen about, a neighbour, a shopkeeper, a friend's boyfriend and I'd feel uncomfortable if I saw them, in case they knew somehow, or had dreamed the same dream. Once it was Leo. I couldn't get away from him, couldn't unstick his lips from mine so I thought I would suffocate. I woke gasping for breath, with the ashy taste of cigarettes in my mouth.

For a while I avoided Spicer, confused and alarmed by my conflicting emotions. No doubt my counsellor would know what to make of it all but I didn't want to tell her. It was silly anyway – me inventing meaning where there was none. I knew what she'd say. Me being bonkers basically.

Spicer met us on the way home one afternoon. He crouched down, held his arms out, and Lucas ran to him, laughing.

'Hey.' Spicer lifted him onto his shoulders, held onto his hands. 'How's my boy?'

'I'm a man,' Lucas said, 'remember?'

'Oops, sorry.' Spicer's laughing eyes caught mine. 'Haven't seen you for ages. How about we go for tea and cake – my treat?'

Lucas bounced up and down on his shoulders. 'Yes, yes.'

'Pearl?'

'Lovely.'

'Yay!' Lucas bounced again, grabbing Spicer's hair.

We sat outside the cafe because the sun was shining. Lucas had a chocolate milkshake with froth on the top. Spicer bought lemon drizzle cake and tea. It was such a lovely day.

Spicer stirred his drink. A cloud moved across the sun. A shadow crossed his face and I saw darkness in him.

'What's wrong?' I said.

'Nothing.' He lifted his face and smiled. Hazel eyes sparkled in the sun – green and gold. Nothing dark about him. Nothing. 'We need to talk, that's all.'

'What about?' He knew. He knew why I'd been avoiding him. Heat rose up my neck.

Lucas sucked the froth of his milkshake through the straw, made a racket. His eyes flitted between me and Spicer, sensing the sudden tension.

'Later.' Spicer nodded pointedly towards Lucas.

'What?' Lucas said. 'What about me?'

'Nothing, little man.' Spicer ruffled his hair. 'Nothing –

just grown-up stuff.'

'I *am* grown up.'

'I know,' Spicer said. 'But you're still a *little* man. This is big man stuff.'

Lucas pouted, sucked extra-loudly on his straw.

'For God's sake stop it!' I said, too sharply.

His huge eyes stared up at me, hurt.

'Sorry.' I tried to catch Spicer's eye but he was looking down the road. It was empty, the road – no cars, no people.

'How about we go to the park?' He turned to Lucas as he said it, even though he must have known I was trying to catch his eye. He *must* have known, and the fact that he didn't want to look at me made me nervous.

What an idiot I was. Why couldn't I have just acted normally? Like he did? As if it didn't matter? Because it didn't. It didn't matter. It was nothing and I'd turned it into some huge problem. You're pathetic, I told myself. A pathetic fool.

I stood. What tea was left in the pot was stewed anyway. My half-eaten cake looked forlorn somehow, alone there in the middle of the plate.

Spicer and I sat on a bench while Lucas played on the slide. There were a couple of other children there, ones I'd seen in nursery. The mothers smiled. I smiled back, I think. I hope. Even though my face felt rigid and hard to move.

It was dusk, and something, maybe the cold grey light or the sharp smell of night in the air, took me right back to being seventeen, to going out for the evening with Abbi and Jess – all of us dressed up, wearing too much make-up, nervous. And I wondered how that girl – that shy, excited, hopeful girl – had turned into me.

Spicer played with a stick, traced the outline of his shoe. He was the one who'd wanted to talk and yet he was saying nothing.

'Well?' I said.

'We have him.'

Tea and sponge cake curdled in my stomach. 'Him?' *Him* could mean anyone, couldn't it? *Him* could be anyone at all.

He dropped the stick and sat forwards, hunched over, elbows on his thighs.

He was nervous, I realised – afraid to tell me, so I already knew who 'him' was, even before he said it.

'Art,' he said.

I could think of nothing to say – nothing.

A sudden gust of wind rustled the branches over our heads. A small whirlpool of brown and red autumn leaves scudded across the play surface. It waltzed across the playground towards Lucas. Sudden fear caught at my throat, as if those leaves were possessed, had a brain, a purpose.

'Just him?' I said. *No Papa? None of the real instigators, the real criminals?*

'For the moment.' He gave me a wary, sideways look. 'I thought you should know.'

'Thank you.'

He sat back, hands resting loosely in his lap. 'I'm going to visit him.'

'Right.'

'Is there anything you want to say?'

'What? To him?'

He nodded.

'Like what?'

He shrugged. 'I don't know.'

Of course he didn't, any more than I did. 'You can tell him I'm doing fine without him. You can tell him he didn't kill me with his lies.'

He lifted a hand, ran it through his hair.

'Actually, I can tell him myself,' I said. 'I'll come with you.' Maybe I didn't mean it, not really. I wanted Spicer to think I was brave, see that I was over it, had moved on.

He stared up at the branches above. 'Not a good idea. He's changed. You wouldn't recognise him.'

He meant the Art I loved no longer existed. Perhaps he never had. Perhaps my counsellor was right. It still made me sad, the idea of him shut in behind bars. It carved a small, hollow ache in my chest.

Spicer shot me a quick glance. 'I shouldn't be telling you this.'

'Who am I going to tell?' I said. The air chilled. I shivered. 'We should get home.'

We walked back in uncomfortable silence. Even Lucas was quiet, slumped over Spicer's head, thumb stuck in his mouth. Spicer dropped him onto the sofa and kissed the top of his head. He stopped as he passed me on the way out. 'You *are* okay, aren't you?'

'Of course.' I gave him my brightest smile and wondered if it fooled him.

9. PEARL

I lay awake for most of the night, trying to picture Art in prison, in a cell like a common criminal. I couldn't do it. He'd always seemed so powerful, untouchable. That anyone would dare to arrest him was a shock. That he'd allow anyone to lock him up was unthinkable.

As the sky began to lighten on the horizon, sleep finally came. Although the alarm woke me at the usual time, my head was muzzy. It made me slow, sluggish, and we were late leaving. By the time we got to nursery, the gates were already locked, doors closed. Lucas clung to my hand. I pressed the buzzer once and waited. The CCTV camera made me self-conscious. I imagined someone inside watching me, sneering at my old, tatty Parka, my scuffed Doc Martens. 'Look at her,' I imagined them saying. 'That poor child doesn't stand a chance,' or, 'No more than a kid herself. Should've had him adopted, let him have a decent upbringing.' And maybe they'd be right. I *was* scruffy. All my clothes, barring underwear, were second-hand, and most of Lucas's too. But I loved him, and that counted for something, didn't it?

'Mummy.' Lucas tugged on my arm.

'Mmm?'

'The lady. She's talking.' He pointed at the intercom.

Then I heard it.

'Hello?' and a sigh, a big one, the kind people do when they're really ticked off.

'Sorry,' I said, and thought how childish I sounded. I was twenty-two for pity's sake, but somehow my age didn't fit.

I'd stalled at seventeen, stuck in a time warp where everyone grew up around me and I just stagnated.

Not the best start to the day, but I cheered up in uni and had a good mark for my latest assignment. By the time I came to pick Lucas up, I was on a high.

Usually he was one of the first children to come out, would come hurtling through the door, clutching whatever he'd made that day. That afternoon though, he didn't appear until last. I managed to suppress the vague twinge of unease in my belly as, one by one, the parents and au pairs left. Panicking before I had anything to panic about wasn't good. Living on my nerves. It wasn't healthy, Mum said, would lead to a build-up of lactic acid – or something – in my muscles. I calmed myself, and watched the door.

A woman I hadn't met before brought Lucas out. She looked smarter than the others, perhaps hoping to make an impression on her first day. More like a model than a childcare worker. Killer stilettos, full make-up. A bit glam for working with mucky toddlers. Crimson red spiky hair, long, shiny, red-painted nails. A health and safety risk, I thought, those nails. As usual Lucas was clutching his latest artwork proudly, his chin lowered, a shy smile dimpling his cheeks.

'He scratched his back,' the woman said. 'Just a small graze.' She ruffled his hair. 'Fell off your chair, didn't you?'

Lucas nodded, mouth pursed.

'We cleaned it all up, and put a small plaster on, but it's nothing.' She put a hand on my arm. 'Barely broke the skin.' There was something odd about her eyes, the flatness of the brown iris, the blank nothingness behind them.

'Right.' Why make such a big thing of it if it was just a scratch? I didn't like her touching my arm, didn't like her eyes, didn't like her nails. I moved away. 'Thank you.' She probably had me down as a neurotic mother. Maybe the others had warned her, said I was a bit . . . I imagined them tapping their temples, lowering their voices . . . a bit touched. That would be it, but it still bothered me, the way she'd held my arm and stared, as if she was checking I'd heard her, checking I believed her.

The evening was taken up with making food, getting Lucas to bed, and researching my new assignment. I didn't think about the scratch again until the following morning. I woke early, and it was the first thing that popped into my head. My stomach tightened. The familiar shot of adrenaline meant there was no hope of getting back to sleep. I got up, made tea, had a shower. I watched the clock, waiting for it to be time to wake Lucas. The minutes went by so slowly, each one crawling by, that I had to check the laptop, thinking the clock must be broken. In the end, I could wait no longer.

I pulled his covers back slowly, holding my breath. I wanted to pull the plaster off without waking him. It was over his spine, just above his hips. A small plaster. I picked at the edge of it with my fingernail.

Lucas jolted upright. It made me jump – caught in the act. Guilty.

'I just want to see your scratch,' I said.

'Why?'

I moved so that I could see his back properly and tried again. It was stuck fast. My nail couldn't even lift the very edge of it.

'Ow!' Lucas squirmed away from me. 'Leave me alone.'

'I can't,' I said. 'I have to see it.' Why I had to see it was as much a mystery to me as it was to Lucas.

I picked at the stupid thing while Lucas grizzled and cried, so I bathed him, soaking the plaster, rubbing it with soap, and still it wouldn't shift. I tried to keep calm but my pulse was thumping in my throat. I called Spicer.

His voice was thick and sleepy. '*What?*' he said, when I told him about the scratch.

'Sorry, but I can't get the plaster off.'

He yawned down the phone. 'Then leave it on.'

'Spicer.'

'What?'

'Nothing.' I was being ridiculous, I knew.

'Look,' he said, 'leave it for now and I'll come over later and get it off, okay?'

'All right.' I ended the call. Lucas shivered.

'Just one more go.' I rubbed the bar of soap over it, lifted the edge of the plastic. 'For pity's sake,' I said. 'How bloody stupid.'

Lucas gasped.

'Sorry.'

'I'm cold.' He whined. 'I want my . . .'

'Shut up.' I had the corner lifted and could see a small patch of red skin. 'Just shut up a minute.' I pulled it, tore the plaster from his delicate skin.

He yelped.

'Okay.' I wrapped him in the biggest, fluffiest towel I had. 'Okay. Sorry, sweetie. I'm sorry.' I kissed his damp hair. 'Mummy had to get it off.'

I dried him, then examined his back. It seemed I'd caused

more damage in removing the plaster than he had in falling off his chair. The graze itself was surrounded by red, bruised skin where the stupid glue or whatever it was had stuck. Once I'd dressed him, I had another look. The skin around it was less inflamed, and now the graze was clear to see. A scratch, nothing more. I turned him to face me, pulled his jumper down, kissed the end of his nose. A fuss about nothing. I felt almost faint. I didn't even know why I'd been so afraid.

He ate his breakfast with a frown. My cheery talk just made him grumpier.

'How did you fall off your chair?' I said.

He shrugged, shoved another spoonful of cereal into his mouth.

'Who put the plaster on?'

He looked up at me with those gorgeous eyes, and I sat back. I felt as if he'd slapped me, as if a physical jolt had hit me. It was as if Art was sitting opposite me – that same terrifying look.

I tried to pick up my tea but my hand was shaking too much. Every part of my body quaked with something, some primeval fear. I stood. 'Just one more look.'

'No-er,' he whined, crossly.

'Please.' I stood him with his back to the window and pulled up his jumper again. It was hard to see. The day was dark and gloomy. There was a definite vertical scratch along his spine – tiny, no longer than my thumbnail. It looked as if there was a horizontal scratch too, even smaller. Was it enough to make a fuss? I stood back, checked it again. It was nothing, barely noticeable.

I held a hand out to Lucas. 'Let's go and see Spicer before

nursery, shall we?'

'Yes!' He jumped up and down.

I strapped him into his car seat without looking at him. How crazy that I was avoiding his eyes. I was afraid of my own child – a little boy – a boy I loved more than anything in the whole universe.

The streets grew scruffier as we drove. Empty, boarded-up shops vied with closed-down pubs, their paint peeling, weathered, faded signs swinging forlornly in the breeze.

We pulled up alongside a terrace of dilapidated four-storey houses. I unclasped the harness, and lifted Lucas into my arms. He said something but the rumble of a passing train drowned out his words.

The communal door was open as usual. We traipsed up two flights of stairs. Spicer had no doorbell, so I knocked. Everything was painted magnolia that had gone a bit grubby at the edges. The tiled floor was dusty.

He took ages to answer the door. When it did finally open, he stood blocking my view, his fair hair sticking up at the back. He was naked from the waist up.

'Can we come in?'

'It's, um . . .'

'Please?'

He stepped aside.

A girl sat in his bed, clutching the quilt to cover herself. She looked about my age, maybe a couple of years older. She was pretty, curvy, very curvy, with long mousy hair and too much black eyeliner. The whole room smelled of sex. I'd forgotten the smell. It hit me how long it had been. Years. Years.

Spicer picked sleep from the corner of his eye and

yawned.

'Sorry,' I said. 'I . . .' I waved a hand about in the air. 'I just wanted Spicer to look at something, but . . .' My words tailed off as a distant rumble grew louder, until the whole room vibrated with the noise. The walls, the floor, everything shook like an earthquake.

Lucas slipped his hand into mine and leaned his head against my leg. He stared at the girl.

She wrapped the duvet around herself.

'Look,' I said, 'I'll come back later.'

'Don't worry.' She shuffled off the bed, keeping the duvet around her like a sarong. 'I've got work anyway.' Her gaze slid to Lucas, then to Spicer. 'Is he yours?'

Spicer shook his head.

'God, no,' I said. 'No – no, we're just friends.'

She nodded. 'Wicked eyes.'

She meant it as a compliment. I knew that, and yet I pulled Lucas close. Why wicked? Why not beautiful, amazing, even awesome? It had to be wicked, didn't it? Had to be.

She bent and picked up her clothes from the floor, then shuffled to the tiny bathroom, trailing the duvet behind her.

I feigned interest in the photos on Spicer's mantelpiece until she'd shut the door, making sure my eyes didn't stray to the bed.

Lucas frowned. 'Why is *she* here?'

'She's my friend,' Spicer said. 'We were having a sleepover.'

'She's – nice,' I said.

'Mmm. So what's up?'

He had his faded old jeans on. Fair hairs curled on his chest, and in a line from his navel to the top of his jeans.

I looked away, felt my face grow hot.

'Will you have a look at it – the scratch?'

He sighed. 'Okay.' He crouched down in front of Lucas, and looked into his eyes. 'So you hurt your back?'

'No.' Lucas shook his head so hard, his hair flew around.

'Mummy said you had a plaster on it.'

'That was yesterday,' Lucas said.

'Can I have a look?'

'No.' Lucas put his hands behind his back.

Spicer's eyes narrowed. 'What if I made it worth your while?'

Lucas frowned.

Spicer went to the kitchen cupboard, opened it, and slipped something into his pocket. 'What if I had a little treat?'

Lucas looked suspicious. 'What treat?'

'Something you like.'

'Chocolate?'

Spicer pursed his lips. 'Possibly.'

'Yes. Yes.' Lucas turned his back and pulled his jumper up.

Another train rattled by, shaking the cups on the work surface.

Spicer crouched down and ran his finger over the scratch. He rubbed his finger and thumb together.

'What is it?' I said.

Spicer glared at me. 'Wow,' he said, loudly. 'You must have been very brave.'

'I was,' Lucas said.

'How did you do it?'

Lucas shrugged. 'It didn't hurt, but the teacher said I had to have a plaster. Then it hurt.'

I held onto the wall. I thought I might die of a heart attack. My chest was so tight – the pain radiated up my neck, pulsing, pushing.

Spicer glanced at me and away, back at the scar. I crouched down too, more to stop myself fainting than anything.

It was tiny – really tiny, but unmistakeable – an inverted cross. Some kind of milky fluid seeped from it. 'What *is* that?'

My pulse banged inside my head, as if my brain wanted to burst through my skull. My chest hurt. I swallowed, but there was no saliva, nothing.

Lucas tried to move away. I held him fast and he began to cry. 'It's okay, little man,' Spicer said. 'It's okay.'

'There – look.' I pointed. 'See that line.' I traced the tiny vertical line with my finger. It was no longer than a couple of centimetres. 'And there.' An even tinier, fine horizontal line crossing it, two thirds of the way down.

'What about it?'

'It's the mark.'

'What mark?' Lucas said.

Spicer stared at me. 'Mark?'

'You know.' I mouthed the word *Mesmeris*.

He scoffed, sat back on his heels. 'It's not. It's nothing.'

'Then what's that stuff – that liquid?'

'What liquid?' Lucas said.

Spicer shrugged. 'A bit of pus.'

I pulled Lucas's jumper down and Spicer gave him the

chocolate. He ran off and sat cross-legged on the sofa.

'You don't think it's . . ?' My throat closed up.

'Pearl. We've both seen the marks, yeah?'

I nodded.

'And they're long, and deep.'

I nodded.

'That's just a scratch.'

'Yes.' I breathed deeply. He was right. Of course he was right. The Mesmeris mark traced the spine almost all the way from shoulders to coccyx. The horizontal line crossed the back from side to side, just above the hips. Lucas's scratch was nothing like it. Nothing like it.

I laughed. 'I'm going insane.'

Spicer wrapped his arms around me. 'What do you mean *going?*'

I felt his big, strong heart beating, felt his warmth, his goodness, and I wanted to stay there forever, to smell his salty skin, feel its softness against my cheek.

The bathroom door opened.

Spicer and I sprang apart, as if we'd been caught out doing something wrong.

'Don't mind me.' The girl sashayed past us and opened the door. 'See ya.'

'Hang on.' Spicer ran out after her. Murmurings came from the hallway.

'Look Lucas.' I pointed at a spider in the corner of the room – a short-legged, black one, his favourites. I chattered about it, loudly, about spiders in general, so as to drown out Spicer's conversation in the hallway. Lucas frowned at me. 'You don't like spiders.'

'No.' I laughed. 'No, I don't, but . . .'

Spicer seemed quite happy when he came back in.
'Sorry,' I said.
'It's fine.'
'What's her name?'
'Tina.' He frowned. 'Or Tia.'
We stared at each other.
'What?' he said.
'Nothing.'
'Don't judge.'
'I'm not.'
'You are. You should see your face.'
'I can't help my face.' I felt furious and tearful at the same time, and was far too aware of the closeness of his body. I held a hand out to Lucas. 'Nursery.'

Only later that night, did it hit me that I had been jealous. I *had* judged them, but it was borne out of envy. Cheap and tacky as it was, I'd never have what Spicer had with Tina/Tia. My life lay before me, empty of kisses, a wasteland.

That night I dreamed Art came into my bed as he used to do. It was so real, the way the mattress dipped under his weight as he climbed in behind me, the feel of his naked body against my back, his hands inside my pyjamas caressing my skin, the touch of his lips on my shoulder. Another kiss sent shivers through my body. He kissed my neck. He kissed behind my ear.

Intense longing overwhelmed me. I turned to kiss him back, and he was gone. A cold, empty bed. I was so certain he'd been there that I got out of bed to look for him. I searched the house – the bathroom, Lucas's room, downstairs, the living room, kitchen. He had to be there.

Had to be, because my skin still burned where he'd touched me. But the doors and windows were locked. The house was empty, except for me and Lucas.

I sat on my bed. Tears poured down my face. I just wanted Art to come back, even if he wasn't real, even if it was a dream. I cried myself into a deep, dreamless sleep that left me dazed and groggy in the morning. Art's visit seemed more vivid than the house, the world outside, even Lucas, so that I wondered which was the dream, and which reality. I wondered which I would choose to be real, if I had the choice.

10. SPICER

Spicer waited impatiently for the results from the lab. He hadn't been permitted to view Malki's DVD himself.

'You're too close, lad,' Jim had said.

In other words, they were afraid it would show his sister's murder and they didn't think he'd cope. Would he? Spicer wasn't sure. Maybe not. The not seeing was almost as bad though. He spent a good few sleepless nights wondering yet again what torment Becky had gone through, imagining all kinds of foul torture. Horrors that made him toss and turn, made him cry out.

In the end, it showed nothing conclusive. Becky didn't appear on the screen, Jim said, although some of her friends did. There were flailing limbs, grainy and blurred. Screams, pleading, laughter. The recording was of such bad quality that the only identifiable perpetrators were people already dead.

'Convenient,' Spicer said.

Jim nodded. 'There's no evidence Art was there – no evidence he wasn't.'

'Brilliant. So we can't charge anyone?'

Jim shrugged. 'Sorry, lad. Not this time.'

Not this time, not ever, Spicer thought. Not that he was surprised. Papa was always one step ahead of them – always. Mesmeris were slippery, impossible to pin down, impossible to convict. He was pretty sure Art wasn't involved in his sister's murder anyway, at least if what Pearl said was true, but he must have known who *was* there that night, who took part in the torture. He could help bring them to justice. All Art had to do was open his mouth, and Spicer was going to make sure he did just that.

He drove around the packed hospital car park. No spaces anywhere. Well, he'd wait. Art wasn't going anywhere. That he was alive at all astounded Spicer, the state he'd been in when they found him. They'd arrived at Pitt's mansion at half past four in the morning to find the place in the care of an elderly woman. She'd opened the front door in a quilted dressing gown and slippers, peering out at them.

She'd rented the house for the winter, she said, with her grandson. No, she'd never met the owner. Yes, she'd rented it through an agency. The name escaped her, she said, with a sweet smile. 'Memory's going.' She tapped her head.

The grandson was out. 'Courting,' she said, 'although I'm not supposed to know.' She shook her head. 'Young people these days.'

Yes, of course they could look around the place. She'd frowned. 'I hope there's nothing wrong.'

'No,' they assured her. 'Just routine.'

A routine visit at half four in the morning.

She claimed to know nothing about the hidden courtyard and Spicer believed her. The horror on her face when they found Art was genuine. No one passes out like that if they're faking it. Poor old girl. Spicer wondered if she'd ever recover from the shock. Sometimes people didn't – not ever.

Finally someone came for their car and he was able to park. The hospital itself was modern, functional, soulless, just like hundreds of others across the country. A faint clinical smell of disinfectant clung to the air.

He showed his warrant card to the copper standing outside Art's room. It seemed strange that they were guarding Art from the world, rather than the other way around, the way it should have been.

Spicer pushed the swing door open.

Art lay with his eyes closed, tubes coming into and out of him like something out of a sci-fi film. His scalp was a mess, chunks of his black hair gone, bloodied patches. That hadn't been there when they brought him in. His skin had a greyish tinge. That meant death, didn't it? He'd been told Art's condition was critical. He looked worse than that.

The door swung shut behind him. He took a step towards the bed. The room was silent save for slow breathing and the rhythmical clicks of the monitors. 'It's Spicer.'

Art's hands lay by his sides – skeletal, pale, the fingertips red raw. He opened his eyes and turned his head. The motion – slow, menacing, made the hairs stand up on the back of Spicer's neck.

He's a man, just a man.

The force of Art's blue eyes hit him with a jolt. Their power was so out of sync with the rest of his appearance, it seemed they didn't belong to the morbid body that housed them but existed independently.

'So.' Art's drawl was just the same – slow, sardonic. 'Here he is, my saviour.'

'I need to ask you some questions.'

A bitter smile. 'You think I'm going to squeal?'

'Why did they do this to you?'

Art shrugged. 'I've been disciplined.' He winced, put a

hand to his head.

'For?'

'Doesn't matter.'

Something buzzed next to Spicer's right ear. He batted it away, felt the back of his hand hit something. He looked up to see it – some kind of flying insect, about five, maybe six centimetres long. It flew hunched, legs dangling. Its narrow, pointed abdomen ended in a sword-like spike that pointed downwards.

'What *is* that?'

'A bug.' Art's lip twitched. It could have been a smile, or an involuntary tic. It was hard to tell.

The bug flew straight back and buzzed in Spicer's ear. He whacked it away. 'For fuck's sake.'

'Forget the insect.' Clipped words, sharp.

The insect buzzed his ear again. Spicer dashed it away and shook his head.

'It's an ichneumon,' Art said, wearily. 'Nothing to worry about.'

Spicer watched it fly up to the ceiling. 'There's something not right about that thing.'

A nurse barged in – big, cheery, like a whirlwind. 'Morning!' She was so loud, it hurt Spicer's ears. She stopped and frowned when she saw Art. 'Have we been at it again then?' She tutted, bustled over to his bed. 'What did I tell you? If you don't leave it alone, it'll get infected and then what, eh?'

Art gave her a look that would make most people quake. Not her. She didn't even seem to notice. She tutted as she swabbed the raw skin, winced when he winced.

'See you had a card from your dad.' A get well card, all

flowers and bluebirds stood on top of the cabinet. 'That's nice.'

Art closed his eyes.

She checked the monitor, noted down the readings. 'Maybe they'll let him visit. That would be nice now, wouldn't it?'

Art snorted.

She stuck a thermometer in his ear, wrote his temperature on the notes. 'That's it.' She patted his cheek. 'Sleep's the best medicine. That's what I always say.'

And then she was gone, all in a rush, just as she'd come in. The room felt empty without her.

Spicer walked over to the cabinet and picked up the card.

You'll be out of there in no time and back where you belong.

Papa

That could mean anything – back as head boy in Mesmeris, or back in the courtyard, shackled to the tree.

'They've left Brighton,' Spicer said. 'Do you know where they've gone?'

Art opened his eyes, rested his head back on the pillow. 'No.'

'They left you there to die.'

'I expect Mrs Arnold would have found me eventually.'

'Not until the smell of your rotting corpse reached her.'

Art made a gurgling sound. It took a moment for Spicer to realise it was a laugh.

'You can have them arrested, locked up,' he said. 'Isn't that what you want?'

'I've been reminded . . .' Art winced, shifted position. 'Reminded where my allegiance lies.' He panted, as if he was out of breath. 'And it's not with you.'

'If we don't know where they are, we can't keep an eye on them.'

Art's eyelids closed.

'You bastard,' Spicer whispered.

Slow, even breaths.

'You must care about your kid, for Christ's sake,' Spicer said. 'They'll come after him and you know it.'

Nothing. No halt in the breathing. 'Just give us *something* – anything.' Art was asleep or unconscious. Spicer shook his shoulder. 'Wake up, you wanker.'

A high-pitched beeping filled the air. A doctor rushed in, followed by a nurse, then more doctors. They elbowed Spicer out of the way. 'Can you leave please?'

Spicer couldn't even see Art through the medics clustered around him.

'Let him go to hell,' he whispered as he left the room. 'Let him go to hell and burn.'

11. PEARL

Lucas's scratch was healing nicely. I felt silly for having made such a fuss about it. Spicer didn't mention Art again so slowly I was able to push him back into the hidden recesses of my brain, at least in the daytime. I even forgot about the accidental kiss eventually. Spicer had a new girlfriend – one with cropped dark hair this time, older than him by a long way. He said he was practising diversity. I said nothing.

He still came over to see us, but not as often. He was working on something with Uncle Jim, he said. I knew it must involve Art, but I didn't ask what was happening and he didn't tell me.

The older girlfriend didn't last long. She decided to go back to her estranged husband and try again.

'Bit of a relief,' Spicer said. 'All she ever talked about was him. How crap he was at this, rubbish at that.'

Precisely what her husband had been crap at he didn't say but I could imagine.

'Feel as if I haven't seen you and Lucas for ages,' he said. Maybe he wasn't as blasé as he made out about the break-up. There was a hint of sadness in his voice, I thought. Then again, it was probably my imagination.

I told him to come over any time he was free, so when the doorbell rang the following afternoon I assumed it was him. My mind was so fixed on the idea of it being Spicer that it took a moment for the two women's faces to register.

'Pearl Miller?' the shorter one said. She was almost as

wide as she was tall, with several chins that wobbled when she spoke.

Something about the way they looked at me made me uneasy. 'Who are you?'

The other woman fished about in her bag. She was tall and slender, with greying black hair in a severe short cut, which emphasised her angular cheekbones, giving her a masculine look. 'We're from social services.'

My stomach flipped.

'Mummy. What's the matter?' Lucas's little voice warbled.

'Everything's fine, darling,' I said, my voice high and fake.

The short one handed me her ID card.

I stared at it without seeing anything. Why would social services want to see me? The card looked official, but how would I know?

'You *are* Pearl Miller, aren't you?' Shortie said.

'Yes.'

'My name's Mel, and this,' She pointed at the taller woman, 'is Velma. Can we come in?'

'It's really not convenient. We've only just got in from nursery. I haven't even had a cup of tea.'

Velma smiled. 'Five minutes, that's all. We'd just like a little chat.'

Panic sparked in every direction, all over my body, so I couldn't even remember how to put one foot in front of the other. If I didn't let them in, if I slammed the door in their faces, they'd only come back. Perhaps they visited all mums – or all single mums – or student mums. It could be something like that. I opened the door.

We all trooped into the living room.

'Why are they here?' Lucas whispered, loudly, hugging Teddy Frank.

'It's nothing, sweetie.' I turned the television off. 'Nothing. Why don't you go up to your room?'

He shook his head, his mouth small and pinched.

'Is that your teddy?' Mel said, in the kind of fake, idiotic voice some people use to kids.

'It's Frank.' Lucas stuck his thumb in his mouth and frowned.

'Go up to your room, Lucas,' I said. 'And close the door.'

He grunted but clambered off the sofa and clomped upstairs, dragging Frank behind him, banging his feet on every step.

I didn't offer the women tea, but stood awkwardly. 'So?'

Mel's bright button eyes scanned the room, stopped at the pile of books on my desk. 'What are you studying?'

'Creative writing.' The tone sounded defensive. I knew it, but couldn't help it.

'Ooh, lovely. I've always wanted to write a book.'

'You should,' Velma said. 'We'd have some tales to tell, eh?' They both laughed.

I bit my lip. They wandered around, picking photos and ornaments from the mantelpiece and windowsill. To stop myself snatching my property from their hands, I sat on the wooden chair and waved a hand in the direction of the sofa. Better to get it over with. 'What's the problem?'

'No problem.' They said it in unison, with identical smiles. Androids, I thought. Velma sat on one end of the sofa. 'We just thought we'd check you're managing okay.'

'I am,' I said, too quickly.

They exchanged a glance. Mel sat too, hands folded in her lap, a fixed smile pasted onto her face.

Velma lowered her voice. 'I'm sure you appreciate we have to keep an eye on people with a history.'

'History?'

'Of mental illness,' Mel said, without losing the smile.

I stood, started tidying my books, putting lids on pens.

'Are you on medication?'

'No.' I couldn't tell who was speaking, and daren't look in case they saw my terror, fury, hatred.

'Lucas's nursery have expressed – concerns.'

My stomach lurched. 'Concerns? What concerns?'

'Please don't worry.' The voice was soft, sympathetic. 'They mentioned he has a wound?' She paused. 'On his back?'

I spun around. 'Yes.' *This wasn't right. This was not right.* 'It happened at nursery. He slipped off a chair.'

They exchanged a glance. Velma raised her eyebrows and smirked. I wanted to punch her.

'They suspect it may be non-accidental,' Mel said.

'*What?*' I couldn't breathe. My heart felt as if it had moved into my throat. 'What are they talking about? It happened *there*.' I tried to lower my voice, but it was impossible. 'It happened there – *there*. They told me about it when I picked him up. Ask him.'

'We will,' Velma said, without her rigid smile slipping. Her face was like a mask – a hideous, grotesque, clown-like mask.

'Lucas.' I yelled it. 'Lucas.'

He appeared on the stairs, thumb still stuck in his mouth.

'Tell these – *ladies*.' My jaw was so tense I could hardly

get the words out. 'Tell them how you scratched your back.'

He stared.

'Tell them.'

'I don't know.' His eyes filled.

'It's all right.' *Shit! Shit! Now I'd frightened him.* 'It's all right, darling. Just tell them what happened.'

Thumb out. 'It didn't hurt.' Thumb in.

My nails dug into my palms.

'Where did you do it?' Mel said, in that same stupid voice.

Lucas pointed at his back.

Velma and Mel laughed.

'No, darling,' I said. 'They mean where *were* you when it happened.'

'Were you here?' Velma said, quickly. 'At home?'

Lucas shook his head. His big eyes slid to me.

'Where were you then?' Mel said. She must have been taught to do that voice, soft, coaxing, unlike my threatening, terse questions.

'In nursery,' Lucas said.

I took huge gulps of air into my lungs.

'Really?' Velma got to her feet. 'Well.' She smiled at me, eyes hard, vindictive. 'Someone's lying.'

'It's not Lucas and it's not me.' I crossed the room without looking at them, went to the front door and opened it. 'If you could leave my house now, please?' I was playing this all wrong, making enemies of them, but I was far too close to punching one or both of them, and that wouldn't be a good idea. Definitely not.

Mel patted my arm as she left. 'We can see you're coping,

don't worry.'

The genuine smile and kind words threw me.

'I am. I have lots of support.' I gabbled, heady with relief. 'My parents, friends.'

'Boyfriend?' Velma said, eyes sharp.

'No – no boyfriend.'

'Pretty girl like you?'

I didn't answer. What could I say? He's a mass-murdering psycho, and he's currently in police custody? Yes, that would put their minds at rest, no problem.

12. PEARL

I was so livid with the nursery that I didn't sleep at all that night. I got up ridiculously early, before it was light, and made Lucas get ready too. We found ourselves outside long before it was due to open, but I was hoping to catch one of the teachers, maybe even the red-haired one, before anyone else turned up. We paced back and forth outside, me practising what to say, imagining their response, and getting myself even more wound up until my stomach was a tight, knotted ball and my hands and feet were all pins and needles. Lucas moaned that he was cold, tired, hungry, thirsty. I flexed my fingers and tried not to snap at him. It had been almost two months since the scratch and in all that time, I hadn't seen the redhead again. That made me nervous. Very nervous.

Mothers and children arrived in ones and twos until finally, the doors opened. Lucas ran straight into the classroom, chattering loudly with his friends. I managed to catch the teacher, Miss Bhatti. I asked if I could see the teacher who dealt with Lucas's scratch.

'Do you know her name?' she said.

'No. No, sorry.' *Why hadn't I asked her name?* 'She's tall,' I said, 'with bright red hair and nails.'

Miss Bhatti frowned. 'Really?' She shook her head. 'I don't recall anyone like that.'

'It was weeks ago,' I said, feeling sick. 'She brought him out to me after all the others had left. She said he'd fallen off his chair.'

Why did she have to stare like that, her face all screwed

up?

'I need to see the head, or whatever she's called,' I said.

'Of course.' Her mouth pinched in at the edges, all crimped like the edge of a pie.

She ushered me into an empty office, and motioned to a plastic chair. I sat and waited.

'Ms Miller.' The well-to-do voice belonged to a woman in her forties, with curly, greying hair. She held out a hand. 'How can I help?'

I explained about the scratch and the woman who'd brought Lucas out to me. She shook her head and pulled an A4 book from the desk drawer.

'That must have been the work experience girl.' She pursed her lips. 'She wasn't very reliable.'

Horrible, sick dread gripped me. 'You let her near my son?'

'She had all the relevant checks, I can assure you. Now, let me just . . .' She leafed through the book. 'We record accidents in here,' she said. 'Everything, from a grazed knee to . . . No. Nothing.'

Fury, frustration and panic fought for control.

'Where's this girl now?'

'I do apologise, Ms Miller. There's no harm done, surely.'

'No harm?' My brain buzzed, thoughts shooting in all directions, except useful ones. 'You complained to social services.' My voice rose. 'About *me*, when the scratch occurred here.' I tapped the desk with my finger. 'Here on this property because you . . .'

'Social services?' she said. 'No. No, Lucas is very well looked after. We have no concerns about him.'

No concerns?

'We certainly didn't contact social services.'

I was so surprised, I think my brain switched off. I stared at her for ages, until she asked me if I was all right, if I needed a drink of water.

'No thank you.' I felt almost drunk as I left the building, my balance all over the place. My shoulder whacked into the doorframe on my way out. Pain radiated down my arm, but it didn't cut through my trance. I wandered home in a daze. I don't think I blinked the whole way.

I rang Spicer. He said it was probably a mistake or some malicious prankster trying to cause me problems.

'Have you made any enemies?' He said it with a laugh, as if the thought was preposterous.

'Only Papa,' I said.

That stopped him laughing at least. 'It's nothing, Pearl. Forget it.'

'Right,' I said.

Forget it. People were always telling me to forget things and I never could. Never could.

13. SPICER

Spicer's dream followed an all-too-familiar path. The same dark woods, the same slaughtered ravens hanging from the branches. Then the buzz, the hum of the blowflies. He knew what was coming, and yet still he looked up. Part of him knew it was a dream, but the horror was as sharp as ever. The gaping hole in the flesh of the throat, the white of the exposed bones, the heaving mass of creamy-white maggots. The smell.

He didn't scream – never did any more.

The dream faded, but the smell didn't. It intensified. Not the usual sour smell of decay, of rotting flesh, but something else. Tobacco. He opened his eyes.

A small, round dot glowed red in the corner of the room. It moved, grew brighter to orange, then yellow, then back to red.

'All right?' The voice was familiar – horribly familiar.

Spicer sat up. His eyes strained to see through the darkness. The red dot moved upwards, glowed brightly again, then faded, but in the glow of it, at the brightest point, he saw a face. A dark figure was silhouetted against the grey of the window. Someone was sitting in the armchair, watching him. Someone he knew. Someone dead. Leo.

A new nightmare, he told himself. It didn't stop the hairs standing up on the back of his neck, didn't stop the shiver travelling across his skin.

'Papa wants to see you,' Leo's voice said.

It wasn't real. None of it was real. Nightmare, that's all.

Just a nightmare. Then why the hell couldn't he wake up? He reached out, switched on the table lamp. Its feeble low energy bulb grew brighter, and still the nightmare went on. Leo didn't disappear. He sat, bathed in yellow light, smoking.

He flicked the ash from his fag onto the lino. 'Need your expertise.'

Spicer coughed, breathed. 'I'm done with all that.'

'You're never *done*.' Leo's teeth flashed white. 'Once you're in, there's no getting out.' He tilted his head back and blew smoke up towards the ceiling. 'D'you ever see that girl? You know, Art's slag?'

'No.' Any remaining sleepiness disappeared. Adrenaline shot through Spicer's system.

Leo was holding the photo of Lucas. Spicer tried to breathe. It was important to keep calm. He knew that. Keep calm. Don't let them sense your fear.

'Bitch tried to kill me. Pushed me in the canal.'

'No shit.' Spicer gripped his hands together to stop them shaking. 'Don't even remember her.'

'Yeah, you do.' Leo leaned forwards, elbows on his knees. 'You remember.' He had the weirdest eyes. Spicer had forgotten how pale they were – an unearthly grey.

Spicer's mouth dried up. He shook his head.

Leo waved the photo in the air. 'This *your* kid?'

'No,' Spicer said. 'No – not mine. My, er, nephew.' He nodded, smiled, felt his mouth wobble.

'Thought your family were dead.'

'Well, yeah. Not actually related. You know, step . . .'

'*S*he had a kid – the slag.' Leo's eyes bored into Spicer's brain.

'Yeah?' Spicer's pulse banged in his temples. 'Wouldn't know.' He stretched his arms over his head, faked a yawn. 'Listen . . .'

'Papa asked him – Art – asked if she'd produced a kid. He said no, so he pulled his nails.'

'What?' Spicer's flesh tingled.

'Yeah. Every one.' Leo examined his own fingers, pursed his lips. 'Still said no.'

'Look, Leo. I really need to . . .'

'Let's have a drink.' Leo pulled a silver flask from his pocket. 'For old times.'

'I'm all right.'

Leo stood, crossed the room in two strides. He gripped Spicer's hair and shoved the neck of the flask into his mouth. 'Drink it.'

Drink or drown, that was the choice. Spicer swallowed – sweet, bitter, thick. A taste he remembered too well. He kept swallowing, trying to breathe, until the flask was empty. Almost immediately, the room seemed to breathe around him, the walls coming closer, then receding. Something buzzed in his ear. He lifted a hand to swat it away, but his hand was heavy. He hit himself in the face and laughed.

Leo laughed too, high and shrill. Lights flashed in the corners of the room like fireworks. That wasn't safe, was it? Fireworks indoors. Not that he cared too much. It was all a dream anyway.

Leo's face loomed above him, floating. His eyes bulged, pale and grey. The pupils dilated, then grew smaller until they were tiny black pinpricks.

'You know you're one of us, mate, don't you?' he said.

'You never stop being one of us, not once you're in.'

'I know.' And Spicer did know. He'd always known. He'd belonged to Papa all along. How had he forgotten how good it felt to be back with them, with the pink stuff?

The buzzing in his ears died down, and he slept like the dead. The first decent sleep he'd had for nearly three years.

14. PEARL

I loved university. While I had my head buried in other worlds, other lives, I forgot to worry. My confidence grew so that I actually spoke up in seminars. At first, I would shake all over after making a comment, expecting laughter, mocking smiles. They never came. They seemed to think my opinion was as valid as anyone else's. It was a totally new feeling for me, and made me happier than I'd been for years.

One November afternoon, just as I was about to doze off in the middle of an unusually uninspiring lecture, my phone buzzed.

My heart lurched as I saw the call was from nursery. I shot out of the lecture theatre, clutching my coat and bag. Possibilities raced through my mind, all bad. Lucas collapsed, Lucas dead, Lucas missing.

'He's feeling a little under the weather,' Miss Bhatti said. 'We think he'd be better at home. Could you come and get him?'

'Is he all right?'

'Just a bit miserable. Nothing to worry about.'

I breathed, exhaled, felt my muscles relax. 'I'll be there as soon as I can.' I ran to the car. Despite her telling me not to worry, I couldn't shake the feeling there was more wrong than she made out. When I got there though, he was obviously fine. His cheeks were a little flushed, and his hair messed up. Probably nits, she said.

Nits I could cope with. Nits were manageable.

The day was bright, but blustery. I felt a strange sort of

euphoria. I was free, had my beautiful boy, and life was good, should be good, would be good. I'd make sure it was, for me and for Lucas.

'Shall we go to the seaside?' I said.

Lucas nodded, managed a small smile.

I called Spicer. He didn't pick up so I left a message, asked if he was free to meet us at the beach.

The car park was in a copse of trees. In the summer, it would be jam-packed, but on a bright winter weekday, it was empty.

'We'll have the whole beach to ourselves,' I said.

His blue plastic bucket and spade were still in the boot – coated in the summer's sand.

'Yay!' Lucas clapped his hands, and ran towards the beach, his little legs seeming to go much too fast.

'Don't run,' I said, even though it was a waste of time. Of course he'd run. He always did. And, as he always did, he fell. He got to his feet, checked his hands, then laughed and ran on again.

If I had to imagine what heaven would be like, it would be like that afternoon – at least the first part of it. Me and my little boy alone on the beach. There was something sweetly melancholy about the place, although I couldn't work out what. Perhaps it was the watery sun, or the clean, salty air, the smell of the ozone. It was warm enough to take Lucas's coat off, but not his jumper. Little people get cold quickly. The water sparkled under a pale, clear turquoise sky - the kind of sky you only ever see in winter. The rhythmic soft hiss of the surf as waves washed over the shore, and the rattle and clatter of pebbles as they were sucked back into the sea worked like a sedative – soothing and calming. It never stopped, the sea, no matter what happened to us, to our lives, it was still there, still pulsing, beating, like a heart, the life-blood of the world.

Maybe it was just that, that it was so beautiful. In a perfect picture, of course, there'd be a daddy. A daddy who would teach Lucas how to build sandcastles, because mine always collapsed. A daddy who'd paddle with him at the water's edge, and make him brave. He'd have to be a free man, of course, and a different one. Even if he hadn't been in custody, Art would hardly be the type to play. He'd have stood, no doubt looking superior, arrogant, bored.

Still, it made me sad that he would never see his little son playing with a bucket and spade. He'd never again smell sea air, hear the crash of waves, feel the sun. They would put him away for good; of that I had no doubt. Whole life tariffs had been designed for people like him – dangers to society. I told myself it was better for Lucas to have no daddy, than to have his real one. Better for me to have no lover, than that one.

Lucas scratched at his head. I searched through his hair. It was so dark, I was sure any little white eggs would be easy to see – and there was nothing. I'd have a proper look later. It wasn't as if the nits were going to harm him. Another few hours wouldn't hurt. I couldn't bear to leave the beach, to go back to our tiny house.

I lay back on the sand and closed my eyes, felt the sun's rays caress my face. I breathed, and relaxed, felt my body become heavy, as if gravity pushed me down. I imagined the earth spinning in space, imagined me, stuck to its surface by some force or other – centripetal, centrifugal – I could never remember which was which. That's what comes of leaving school early, of being a young, single mother – things like centrifugal force don't really matter in the day-to-day struggle to pay the bills.

Lucas started grizzling, moaning about worms in his head. I sat up. The world looked cold and grey, although the sun still shone as brightly as before. Behind Lucas, far away in the dunes, I thought I saw a movement, a flash of khaki.

My heart felt as if it jumped into my throat. 'We need to go now,' I said.

'Don't want to.' Lucas pouted.

I grabbed his coat and shoved his arms into the sleeves. The temperature had plummeted anyway and the afternoon was spoiled. Lucas began one of his high-pitched cries.

'Shush.' I picked him up, held him to my chest. 'I'll get rid of the nits when we get home, okay? Promise.'

Another deafening wail, right in my ear.

'And you can have ice-cream. How about that?' Last resort of the crap parent – bribery.

Silence. He stared into my eyes, as if to check I meant it, then nodded. 'They're not nits,' he said. 'They're worms.'

'Right.' I stumbled over the rocks. 'Okay.'

I glanced behind us – nothing, no movement. Plenty of places to hide though, behind the tussocks of grass – grass that was khaki in colour. Stupid idiot. How long would it take before I stopped imagining him everywhere, spoiling every outing? I plonked Lucas on his feet and laughed, delirious almost with relief.

Lucas frowned. 'What are you laughing at.'

'Nothing,' I said. 'Mummy's being silly. I thought I saw

someone, that's all.'

'Do you mean that man?' He pointed behind me.

Everything stopped. Even the birds stopped singing. Everything disappeared except my baby's face.

A voice behind me. A voice I knew. 'So, we meet again.'

It was a nightmare, surely. My conscience playing tricks on me.

But there he was, with his sandy hair and his weirdly pale eyes. I could smell him – the distinctive aroma of his cigarettes, sweet and woody.

Lucas clung to my hand, pressed himself against my leg.

'Don't panic.' Leo held his hands out, palms up. 'No blade.' He smiled a reassuring smile. 'This time.'

Then I was back in the church with Jack's lifeblood spurting from his chest, flooding over my legs, over the flagstones. So much blood. And the smell – the sickly-sweet, metallic stench of death.

Leo's mouth contorted, ugly, obscene. 'Your mate. The blonde – remember her? What was her name now? I forget.'

Abbi? Why bring her up now? She was in university somewhere – Loughborough or Leeds or somewhere beginning with L. She was far away - safe.

'She put up a fight, I'll give her that,' he said.

A fight? Abbi, bright, fiery, funny Abbi, fighting? For what? And even as my slow brain began to understand, it shied away. No, they'd have told me. I'd have known. The last time I'd seen her, she'd been sitting on Leo's lap, dressed in her short, red dress. He'd had his hand on her thigh, sliding up her skirt. *Oh, my God! Oh, my God!*

A scream cut through the fog in my head, and Leo

snatched Lucas from my grasp. He turned to run, the bastard, the dead man. He turned to run away with my child.

He shouldn't have touched him. He should never have touched my boy.

I caught the hood of his Parka, yanked him back. I was vaguely aware of Lucas falling, rolling away.

'Hide,' I screamed. 'Hide, Lucas.'

The top of Leo's head hit my jaw as he fell backwards, and then I had him, had him in a headlock. I knew I couldn't let go, couldn't loosen my hold or . . . He tried to get his balance, but I dragged him backwards, jabbing at his face. His hands clutched at my arm, reached back for my head, my face.

Screaming filled the air – mine, his, maybe Lucas's too.

I didn't even know I had the keys in my hand until I saw the blood.

No. No. I let him go, a shudder of disgust, of horror.

He fell to the ground, screaming, clutching at the bloody mess that was his face. A surge of terror washed through me at the realisation there could be others watching, waiting.

'Lucas.' Maybe they'd taken him, the others, while I . . .

'Lucas.' He was nowhere. '*Lucas.*' I ran, darting this way and that, looking behind tussocks, into dips in the sand. 'Lucas.' I screamed it until my voice was hoarse.

And then I saw him, curled in a tight ball, thumb in his mouth, eyes tightly shut. 'Thank God.' I bent down and lifted him. 'It's all right,' I said, already running. 'It's all right, baby. The nasty man's gone.'

I held his warmth tightly to me, cradled his head with

my hand as I ran.

Maybe the others were behind us or waiting by the car. I slowed my pace as we drew near to the trees. A wave of nausea gripped me. *Don't think about the blood, the damage. Not yet. No time.* I peered around the tree.

Two cars parked in the clearing – mine, and Leo's battered red Fiesta.

With shaking hands, I unlocked my car and strapped Lucas into his car seat.

'Mummy?'

'Shush.' I climbed into the driver's seat, slammed the door.

A little voice from the back. 'Who was that man?'

'What?'

'The man you didn't like.'

'Um . . .' I turned the key in the ignition. 'He's er, he's . . .' I released the handbrake, jolted forwards, and stalled. 'Shit!' He wouldn't have been on his own. There'd be others, waiting to ambush us. I pressed the central locking, heard it click home. I turned the key again. The engine raced. 'Crap!' First gear. Where the hell had first gear gone?

'Mummy.'

The note of panic in Lucas's voice sent an electric shock through me. I stalled again then, finally, the engine roared. The tyres spun wildly, before they gripped the surface. I raced along the rutted track, churning up clouds of dust.

'Mummy,' Lucas shouted, cross. 'Who was the man?'

'I don't know, all right?' Blood on my hands, on the steering wheel. Blood everywhere.

The track opened onto a road. I kept an eye on the rear-view mirror, almost drove into a tree, swerved to avoid it and over-corrected, veering onto the opposite carriageway. 'Shit! Shit!'

Lucas started whining. I couldn't take it, couldn't take the noise.

'Shut up. Shut up, Lucas, please.' I pulled out onto the main road, forcing a car to swerve to avoid me. Horns blared. If I didn't calm down I was going to kill us both, do Leo's job for him. 'Sorry, darling.' I breathed, in, out through my mouth. I eased my foot off the accelerator.

'Was he bad, Mummy?'

Where to go? The police? My parents?

'Mummy?'

'*What?*' It came out more sharply than I intended. I saw his bottom lip tremble in the rear-view mirror.

'The man, was he bad?'

'Yes. I mean, no – no. He was just being silly.' I hadn't meant to take his eye out. No, that was a lie. I had meant to. I hoped I'd taken both. 'He was playing a game.'

'Did you hurt him?'

'Gosh, no,' I said, with a feeble laugh. 'He's fine. Right as rain.'

'Oh, good,' he said, his voice wobbling, 'Because I don't want you to go to prison.'

'I won't, sweetie.' Would I? I had no idea. I forced a smile. 'We were just playing. Pretending, that's all.' But would I go to prison, or worse, back to hospital? If I told them it was Leo, who would believe me? They'd lock me up for sure, take my boy away. Mesmeris would know where Lucas was. He'd be in even more danger. An even worse thought occurred to me – that it hadn't been Leo at all, that I'd had a psychotic episode, that the blood all over me, all over the steering wheel was some innocent visitor out for a walk, that I was really truly insane.

A cold sweat broke out all over me. It *had* been him, and he'd told me about Abbi.

Tears ran down my face. I hoped I'd killed him. I really hoped I had. For Abbi. For my friend.

I drove home, because there was nowhere else to go. The first thing I did was wash my hands. Blood. So much blood, swirling around the sink. Had I done enough damage to stop him? He'd never be able to drive, of that I was sure. Maybe he'd die out there on the dunes, if no one found him. Would anyone find him? Shit! Shit!

I called Spicer. He didn't pick up so I left a message asking him to ring back. 'Something's happened. Please, *please* call me.'

Lucas stood in the doorway, his accusing eyes staring straight at me. I did it for him – had to do it for him, and there he was, staring at me as if I was supposed to do something about it.

'For God's sake,' I said. 'Go and watch TV or something.'

He stalked stiffly over to the television and sat in front of it, his back rigid.

'You mustn't tell anybody about the man. It's a secret, okay?'

He nodded, thumb stuck in his mouth.

If someone found Leo . . . Maybe it would rain. I peered out of the window. Grey clouds massed on the horizon, but they were a way off yet. Please – please God, please let it rain. Please don't let anyone find him.

I'd have to go back, make sure he was . . . I heaved.

Pointless. I'd never be able to do it, not in cold blood. I'd just have to hope – what? There was no outcome I could pray for – none, except that it had never happened, that it was a nightmare, nothing more. I changed, stuck my clothes in the washing machine and wiped my Doc Martens with bleach, even though they seemed unmarked. Then I took a cloth and bleach out to the car. The blood smudged over the steering wheel told me it was no nightmare, told me no miracle was going to happen. I cleaned the car, inside and out.

Later, I bathed Lucas. The scratch was barely visible any more. Nothing. Nothing at all. It seemed such a stupid thing to have worried about, compared to Leo and the beach.

'I don't like it when you're cross.' Lucas's mouth turned right down at the corners. 'You're scary.'

'Oh, sweetheart.' I lifted him out of the bath and wrapped him in the best towel, the fluffy, soft one. 'I'm sorry.' I hugged him close and kissed his wet head. 'Don't be frightened of me. I love you more than anything, more than my own life. I just didn't want the man to pick you up, do you understand?'

He shook his head.

'I was afraid he wanted to turn you into a bad man, but you're going to be a good man,' I said, 'like Grandpa.'

'Like Spicer?'

'A bit like Spicer, maybe – yes.'

He smiled. A weak, wan smile, but better than nothing.

'So will you stop worrying now?'

'Yes,' he said. 'I'm going to be a superhero!' He ran into the bedroom, the towel falling away. 'Yay!' he yelled.

As soon as he lay down, he fell asleep. His black hair stood out against the once-white sheets I'd accidently turned grey. Everything in the little box room, everything in my life, was tired and dirty except him, with his pink skin, and his clear blue eyes. He was shiny and new, whilst I fitted well with the furnishings. Washed out at twenty-three.

He stirred, flung an arm over his head, and I thought how small his fingers still were, how soft and delicate his skin. How would I ever be able to protect him from the evil in the world?

15. PEARL

I went downstairs and poured a glass of wine. I was surprised at how well I was coping, all things considered. No panic, no fuss. My phone rang. Spicer.

'Sorry,' he said. 'I had a game.'

At the sound of his voice, my throat closed up, my eyes stung. It was real – Leo, the blood, Abbi.

'What's wrong?' he said.

'Something's happened.'

'What?'

I shook my head as tears spilled down my face.

'Is it Lucas?' He had his gentle voice on – the understanding one.

My 'No' was squeaky, high-pitched.

'Okay.' I heard him move. 'It's okay. I'll be there. Just . . .' There was a bang and clatter. 'Shit.' More noise. 'Just stay there. I'll be two minutes.'

I nodded and the phone went dead. He wasn't two minutes though. It was sixteen minutes and thirty-one seconds before he knocked on the door. I still had the phone in my hand. He let himself in, shut the door behind him and locked it. Then he took one look at me, and dropped his sports bag on the floor.

'What is it?' His arms enveloped me. 'What's happened?'

'Leo,' I said, and closed my eyes so I didn't have to see his face, see his reaction. He said something but I talked over him, had to get the words out before I changed my mind. 'I know you won't believe me, but he tried to take Lucas.'

'Is he all right – Lucas?'

I nodded. 'He's asleep.'

Spicer was quiet. I opened my eyes, but still didn't dare look at him.

'It was Leo. It *was* him, and I hurt him. The, er . . .' I shook my head. 'The blood, it was . . .' I stared at my right hand and shuddered. 'I had my keys . . .' I turned my hand, palm upright. 'I stabbed at his face. I think – I think I blinded him, or maybe – maybe I killed him, I don't know.'

'Did Lucas see?'

'No. No, he was hiding.' I risked a look at his face. 'It *was* Leo.'

'I believe you.'

I thought I must have misheard, but he smiled, his eyes warm – amber and gold and green. 'I believe you,' he said again. I watched his mouth form the words and I kissed it.

It was my fault that it happened. I was the one who pressed my lips to his. I was the one who moved my hands under his clothes, over his warm skin. I was the one who pressed my body against his, who wouldn't let him go until he kissed me back, until I felt his body react, felt his grip tighten around me.

I dragged him upstairs and closed the bedroom door. I stripped his clothes off. He was beautiful, a Greek god, a sculpture that moved, breathed, loved. I couldn't wait. We fell onto the bed, our mouths glued together. I couldn't wait, couldn't, but he slowed me down. He didn't take risks, Spicer. Always prepared, always careful. He whispered things in my ear, things I knew weren't true, that I was beautiful, perfect. He made me feel, for the first time in my life, that I was something precious. He knew how to move, how to make my body sing, and it did. It left me breathless.

Afterwards, he lay on his back.

I ran my hands over his body and only then did I think about how he carried condoms wherever he went. Only then did I think about all the other girls he'd had. All the beautiful blondes, brunettes, redheads with their perfect, no-doubt hairless bodies. I hadn't even shaved my legs, because I wasn't expecting . . .

I pulled the duvet over me, over my stretchmarks, my hairy legs, my saggy bits, and I hoped he'd kept his eyes closed, hoped he hadn't seen me.

'Cold?' he said, with a sideways look, a small smile.

'A bit.'

He put his arm around me, pulled me close.

'Sorry,' I said.

'What for?'

'Seducing you.' Me, a seductress!

'You've been doing that for years,' he said. 'I'm not complaining.'

I raised my head to look at him, but his eyes were closed.

'It won't change things, will it?' My biggest fear. 'Between me and you?'

'Of course not.' He yawned.

'Good.'

'We'll forget it ever happened,' he said, his voice slow and sleepy, 'if it makes you happier.'

'Yes,' I said, because I didn't want him to feel I'd trapped him, didn't want him to feel obliged.

The next morning, the three of us had breakfast together. Lucas's excitement at Spicer being there successfully camouflaged any awkwardness between us. He talked non-stop until Spicer left for work – chatter, chatter, chatter.

'I'll stay over,' Spicer said, under his breath, as he was leaving. 'Until we know where Leo is. Just to make sure.'

He'd sleep on the sofa, he said. Good, said my mind. Not if I can help it, said my body.

It brightened my day, knowing he'd be back later that night, knowing Lucas and I wouldn't be alone. Maybe I should have felt guilty about the sex, but I didn't. My body still tingled from Spicer's touch, and I couldn't feel bad about it no matter how I tried. I still loved Art, adored him, but it was a different love – older, darker. Spicer and Art existed in different worlds, like sun and moon. The me who loved Art wasn't the same me who had slept with Spicer. It was separate, other, therefore it wasn't a betrayal. That's what I told myself.

16. SPICER

Spicer's enquiries into Leo had come up with precisely nothing, just as he'd expected. No dead bodies reported. No hospital admissions that would fit either. He knew Mesmeris had their own team of health professionals, but a blinding would need hospital admission for certain. He imagined Pearl had done less damage than she thought and that meant Leo was out there, angrier than ever, and even more dangerous.

It gave him an excuse to stay at Pearl's at least. He'd sworn things wouldn't change between them, but they had. All the other girls had been pale imitations – something to stop him thinking of her, stop him wanting her. He'd always known that, deep down. When had he fallen for her? That first night maybe, when she stood at the top of the stairs and frightened the crap out of him. Perhaps it was then. Perhaps later. Whatever, it was going to be hard to kid himself they were just friends, but he'd try, for her.

There was no doubt in his mind now that Leo was alive, but finding him would not be easy. Routine paperwork piled up all day, but he couldn't think of anything but Pearl, how to keep her out of trouble with Leo, Mesmeris, the police, how to make her fall in love with him instead of that sick psycho, Art.

He left work early and jogged towards the car park. He was within arm's reach of his car when a black saloon drew up alongside him. The front passenger door swung open and a guy got out. Dark, weasly, with greasy hair. Malki.

'Hop in.' He opened the rear door.

'I'm . . .' Spicer waved a hand in the direction of his car.

'Can't go back without you, man,' he said. 'Papa's orders.'

In other words, he had no choice.

Malki climbed in after him, so he was sandwiched between him and a tall skinhead he'd never seen before. Skinhead didn't look at him, just stared straight ahead at the back of the driver's head, at her dyed crimson hair.

'All right, Ruby?' Spicer said.

She caught his eye in the rear-view mirror. 'Like old times.'

'Yeah.' Except in old times he'd been one of them, not the bloke sandwiched in the back. The last one he'd seen in that position had ended up a victim – a sacrifice at the sabbat.

They drove for miles. No one spoke. Ruby tapped her long, red-painted nails on the steering wheel as though listening to some inaudible music. The sound made Spicer's fingertips itch, but he didn't want to make any enemies – not if he could help it, not yet.

They drove into a gateway, bounced along the uneven drive, until they came to a clearing. A huge, dilapidated house stood ahead of them.

Spicer's mouth dried up. Was this going to be where he ended up? A decayed manor house? A crumbling mansion, like something out of a Victorian ghost story?

The place was almost derelict. Spicer looked up at the roof, at the chimneys, at the ravens circling and croaking above.

The rain started spitting. Malki opened the front door. 'Don't keep 'im waiting.'

They made their way down the hallway. From a closed door to the right came sounds of a low chuckle, and moaning.

'At it again,' Ruby said.

Skinhead smirked. 'Never shuts up.'

A shrill screech echoed down the hallway.

Spicer's stomach clenched. Saliva rushed into his mouth. He swallowed it down. He was not going to throw up in front of these bastards – ever.

They walked down the hallway. He focussed on the tiled floor, a mosaic of unlikely-looking birds and flowers. At waist height all along the wall, ran a moulded plaster frieze of exotic animals – lions, elephants, snakes. Some chipped, some missing altogether. Don't think about the danger. *Think about anything but that.*

A warm glow emanated from the room on the far right. Leo emerged – a scarred, damaged Leo. Red scratches and weals ran across his left cheek, from temple to jaw. His mouth was cut, blackened, bruised. A black patch covered his left eye. The lower lid of his right drooped, pulled away from the bloodshot eyeball.

Pearl had done *that?* Leo had hated her for as long as Spicer had known him, but now? Now his hatred would know no bounds, and that frightened Spicer. She should have killed him, finished the job. Now she was in more danger than she'd ever been.

'Welcome home.' Leo's mouth, swollen and torn, expanded into what could have been a friendly smile, a sneer or a snarl. The latter two seemed more likely.

Ruby nudged Spicer in the back. 'I know you fancy him, darling, but get a shift on, there's a good boy.'

Spicer dragged his gaze away from Leo and knocked at the door in front of him, even though it was ajar.

'Come.' Papa stood behind his desk. He smiled, held out his right hand. 'Welcome, welcome. Come in. Come in.'

Spicer shook Papa's limp, damp hand. It reminded him of a frog he'd once held. He'd forgotten how inky black and empty his eyes were. It was like staring into oblivion, an endlessly dark, cold abyss. His smell too, he'd forgotten – that woody, oily scent. At one time he'd quite liked it but now it made his guts squirm. He suppressed a shudder. Leo came in behind him, closed the door and stood, his back to it, blocking his exit.

Papa's eyes held Spicer's. 'It's been a long time, no? What is it?'

'Almost four years.' Spicer bowed his head. He didn't intend to. It just happened.

'You may have noticed an absence of presence.' Papa glanced pointedly around the room, and back to Spicer with a smug smile.

Spicer waited.

'Art,' Papa said. 'He is no longer with us.'

A trick. It had to be.

'I know. I visited him.'

'Yes. Yes, you did.'

Spicer exhaled. He'd made the right choice. Now it was essential to keep his body language right, hands still, muscles relaxed, as if he'd been on Papa's side all along, as if he had nothing to fear. He sat in the plush red velvet armchair at Papa's signal. The skin on the back of his neck prickled, knowing Leo stood behind him, alert for any movement, any word or sign from Papa.

'How is he? Art?' Papa said, sitting back behind his desk.

Spicer shrugged, kept his shoulders loose. 'Sick. They say he's insane – deranged.'

'And you? What do you say?'

'I think they're right.'

'Mmm.' Papa nodded. 'His mother went the same way.' His eyes glistened in the firelight as if he was about to cry.

You're completely insane, Spicer thought. A nutjob.

'It's sad,' Papa said. 'Very sad.' He shook himself. 'With care, he will be himself again, I am sure.'

You did it to him, you poisonous viper, and now you're getting sentimental?

'His mother mocked me, you know.' Papa pulled a handkerchief from his pocket and dabbed at his eyes. 'When I was a boy.'

It was difficult to imagine anyone mocking Papa, impossible to imagine him as a child, to imagine him as anything other than the narcissistic monster he'd become.

'She and her sister, Jack's mother, they underestimated me.' A sly smile crossed his lips. 'I had my revenge of course, on both of them. I took their children.' He chuckled.

Spicer felt sick.

'I have endless patience, Spicer. Endless. I will wait forever to get revenge, but I *will* get it. I always get it.'

'I'm sure you do.' Prison wouldn't stop this lunatic, Spicer realised. All the years spent trying to bring him to justice were a waste of time. Only death would stop him. Only death.

'We had Art as a toddler.' Papa's smile was sad, wistful. 'He was wonderful. Wonderful. So easy to teach, so emotionless.' He fixed his gaze on Spicer. 'Perhaps we need to go back to taking small children, instead of recruiting these . . .' His lip curled. '. . . so-called *disaffected* teenagers. What do you think?'

'I, er . . .' Was this yet another test? Spicer swallowed. 'I think, er . . .' Sweat sprang out on his forehead.

Leo stepped forward, alongside Spicer's chair, a look of glee on his face. 'Yes, Papa, yes. I've already . . .'

'How would you like to become an Elite, Spicer?' Papa said, as if he hadn't heard Leo, hadn't even seen him. As if he didn't exist.

Leo's face paled. 'What? *Him?*' He jabbed a shaking finger at Spicer, almost touching his cheek.

'Leonard,' Papa said without looking at him, his eyes still on Spicer. 'A drink for our guest, I think.'

'But Papa, *I* should be an Elite, not *him*.' Leo's face flushed purple. A vein throbbed in his neck. 'He's a nobody – *nobody*. I've been loyal. I've stayed with you. I've . . .'

Papa stood, took a step around the desk. 'Get.' Another step. 'A drink.' One more step. 'For our guest.' Another step and Leo cowered. 'I'd do it now if I were you, Leonard, before I make an example of you.'

Leo turned to the door. Firelight glinted off the tears on his face.

'Imbecile,' Papa sneered before the door closed. 'Leonard's becoming a liability, don't you think?' His black eyes stared into Spicer's. 'We should dispose of him, yes? What do you say?'

Get rid of Leo, the one who posed the most danger to Pearl, to Lucas? In theory, Spicer should have been all for it. 'I – perhaps he'd be more use to us alive, since the police are convinced he's dead.'

'Correct answer.' Papa clapped his hands and chuckled.

It had been a test? Shit! Sweat sprung out on Spicer's forehead, tickled as it ran down his temple.

Leo came back through the door with a silver tray. On it stood two crystal tumblers and a bottle of scotch. As he turned to leave, his red-rimmed good eye shot a look of pure hatred at Spicer.

'It's a great honour, no?' Papa said.

Spicer realised Papa was addressing him. 'Yes – yes.' The door slammed. 'I'm . . . Thank you, Papa.' No way, Spicer thought. No way was he going anywhere near becoming an Elite, but for now he had no choice but to play along.

He sniffed at his glass, wondered if Leo had poisoned it somehow. It smelled okay, looked dry. Papa poured the golden liquid into the glasses, handed one to Spicer and raised his own.

'Here's to your rebirth into a new family.'

Spicer sipped at the spirit, felt it burn as it went down, felt the warmth spread from his stomach. He began to relax, despite himself. He tried to fight it, but there was something comforting about being included in Papa's family, warped and twisted as it was. He'd worry about the Elite bit later. He'd get out of it somehow.

Papa poured more scotch into Spicer's glass, held it up. 'Perhaps you're wondering what your first target will be?'

The thought of having a target hadn't occurred to him. 'I suppose so, yes.'

Papa leaned across the desk, lowered his voice conspiratorially. 'It's the child.'

Spicer coughed. 'The . . ?'

'Art's child.' Papa's mouth gaped. Blackness like the gateway to hell.

'I . . .'

'All is in motion.' Papa leaned back in his chair. 'You'll be required towards the end – just to keep the mother out of the way. We need to implicate her, obviously. I've laid the foundations. Social services already suspect she's unbalanced.'

Spicer focussed on the desk, tried to keep his mind a blank. He couldn't afford to think about it, not with Papa sitting right in front of him.

'Perhaps we can find a way to draw some blood from the child. What do you think, Spicer? A few drops spattered about her living room would be enough for forensics, wouldn't it?'

'Yes – yes, it would be enough.' And with her history, no one would ever believe she was innocent.

'If she has no alibi and the child vanishes, well . . .'

Spicer forced himself to look into Papa's eyes. 'Brilliant, Papa,' he said. 'Brilliant.'

'Good.' Papa opened a drawer in his desk and pulled out a flask. 'Calls for something a little more special, I think, to celebrate.'

Spicer gazed at the pink, thick liquid as Papa poured it into his glass. There was no way out, nothing he could do.

Papa passed it across the desk. 'Drink.'

Spicer stared into the abyss, and did as he was told. As he held the sweet, bitter liquid in his mouth he uttered a silent apology, to Jim, to Pearl, to Lucas, to everyone, for what he might do.

The familiar lights flashed at the periphery of his vision.

Everything moved – the paintings, the curtains, the walls themselves. He closed his eyes, surrendered.

Someone put their arms under his and he was lifted into the air. 'Where're we going?'

A voice in his ear – a girl's voice. 'You'll see.' He tried to turn to see who it was but didn't have the strength and then cold air hit him. Voices. Or were they in his head? Lights – lights all around and music. Some kind of classical stuff – melancholy and haunting. Maybe he'd died in his sleep. Maybe this was heaven, but it was dark when the lights went out, and heaven wasn't dark. The music made his head ache.

'I'm . . .' He was thirsty, so thirsty. 'I feel . . .'

He woke lying face down on something hard and cold. Night air blew over his skin. He was naked – outside. He turned his head to see black skeletons of trees against an indigo night sky. The air smelled of damp leaves and earth. He tried to get up, but his hands wouldn't move. They were tied around the stone slab.

An altar. The realisation hit him. He was the sacrifice. All that talk of becoming an Elite was a trick. The inevitability of it almost made him laugh. Voices told him they were standing around him, but none in his eyeshot. If they'd just get on with it, get it over. The chill from the stone went through to his bones. A sabbat, so perhaps he'd escape the drawn fingernails. That would take too long, surely.

Cold, blue moonlight played over the damp grass. Leaves tumbled over each other. Black branches swayed. Silence. Deathly silence.

Perhaps they'd left him there to die. He discounted the idea as soon as he thought it. There was no excitement in that, no spectacle.

Footsteps, voices. Again he tried to turn his head. Again he failed.

Papa appeared in front of him and smiled. 'You are awake, my son.'

'Yes, Papa.' His words were slurred.

'Then we shall begin.' Papa chanted Latin words that spun in Spicer's head. He closed his eyes, lulled by the rhythm of the words. Music played. It sounded ethereal, heavenly. Spicer let himself relax. Whatever happened was out of his control now. It was almost a relief.

Slow drumbeats began, strengthening as the music faded. They grew faster, louder, until the altar below Spicer vibrated. The whole earth seemed to vibrate to the beat. Excitement coursed through Spicer's body. Elation. The ropes around his arms were loosened.

He turned his head.

A boy's face, upside down. Black tape covered his mouth. He grunted, writhed, eyes desperate. Spicer knew those eyes from somewhere. He'd seen them before. At the station. Photographs stuck on the wall. The lad they'd been searching for, Danny. The one who'd gone missing from Pearl's village.

Spicer tried to move, but his limbs refused to obey.

'No,' he shouted. The word was lost in the cacophony of sound. 'No.'

The drums stopped. Silence.

A knife, long and slender, glimmered in the moonlight. It flashed through the air. Dark blood gushed out, splashed over Spicer's back, warm against his skin. 'No.' Tears blurred his vision for a moment, then fell, revealing

Danny's face, his eyes as they clouded over.

Cheers, applause, roars of approval filled the air.

Papa's voice rang out. 'Silence.'

A hush descended. Something tickled down Spicer's spine, from just below his shoulders, right down to his backside. It stopped and then started again, just above his hips, across his back from left to right. It itched and tickled.

'No.'

Something was stuffed in his mouth. He gagged. He was going to die, vomit. A sharp stab in his right buttock and he knew nothing more.

17. PEARL

I tried not to get excited about Spicer coming over. I made a casserole – nothing out of the ordinary. He was just making sure Leo didn't find us, that was all. Still, it would be good to have adult company in the evening for a change.

The delicious smell of chicken and vegetables filled the house. I bathed, shaved my legs, wore my best underwear – silky things Lydia had bought me after I had Lucas. They were still in the packaging, labels attached. On top, I wore my normal clothes – jeans and jumper. I didn't want to look as if I'd made an effort, didn't want to frighten him off.

He'd texted at five and said he would be leaving work shortly and just had a couple of things to do on his way. *Won't be long x*

I liked the *x* after the *Won't be long.* He'd never done that before, never put an x. It made me smile so my jaw ached. I rushed around tidying, even though I'd done it ten times already.

I gave Lucas his food and got him ready for bed.

Six o'clock came and went, then seven. I texted Spicer, asked him what time he thought he'd get to us. No reply.

Lucas whinged and grumbled.

'He'll be here soon,' I said, peering out of the kitchen window for his car.

Half past seven, eight o'clock.

More whining, more tired grizzling from Lucas.

'I don't know *where* he is,' I snapped, 'okay?'

I ate my dinner while Lucas fell asleep on the sofa. I carried him up to bed. Spicer had been held up in work no doubt. Police officers always worked late. I'd seen enough TV cop shows to know that.

I texted him again. No reply.

Perhaps he'd gone to the rugby club on his way. Perhaps he regretted the night before. Maybe he didn't know how to tell me it was a mistake, that he'd only done it out of pity. As the hours passed, I imagined him drinking pint after pint with his mates, trying to think up an excuse, something that wouldn't hurt me. I imagined him confiding in his friends, imagined them laughing, telling him to man up, to tell me straight. Maybe he'd gone back to his place with some random girl instead. Maybe he was, right then, making her body sing, just as he had mine.

That was fine. It wasn't as if we were in a relationship after all.

I went to bed. Alone again.

18. SPICER

A ringing sound woke Spicer, loud, rhythmical, insistent. He opened his eyes. They hurt. The lids dragged, dry and sticky, over his eyeballs. He looked to his right. Shit! That killed. He turned his body instead – easier, slightly.

Blessed silence.

He eased himself to a sitting position, and rested his head back against the wall. Everything ached – his back, his neck, his limbs. He ran his tongue over furry teeth.

The ringing started again. It seemed to come from all corners of the room. Lots of ringing, some low, some high, some screeching. He felt under his pillow, found his phone. Three missed calls. Pearl, the boss, Pearl again.

He stood, slowly, bit by bit. His head swam. The room moved around him, making him queasy. One step at a time, he crossed the room to the kitchen area.

He turned on the tap and filled the kettle. The water hit it like a waterfall, splashing, hammering against the base, against the sides. He closed the lid. The click hurt his ears. A press on the switch and a tiny, unearthly blue light flickered into life. He stared at it. It was moving. He bent down, peered more closely, then jumped back. Shit! There was something in there, inside the light, watching him. He stepped back, heart pounding, while the kettle roared, filling his head with noise.

A fever. It had to be a fever, what with the nightmare, the hallucinations. He swallowed a couple of painkillers and gazed out of the window at reality. Houses, lights, civilisation. Above the rooftops, the sky seemed lighter –

dusky grey instead of the blue-black directly above. Not long until dawn, maybe. He glanced at the cooker – twenty past five. The world would soon come alive, be light again, feel safe again.

Light, that was what he needed. He switched on the ceiling light, blinked in the harsh glare. The kettle clicked. He picked it up, poured the boiling water into his cup. The tea bag floated around, trailing a brown stain that spread like blood. Spicer squeezed the bag, threw it in the sink and sniffed the milk. Not sour, so he added a splash to the tea, stared at the black dot spinning round in his cup. Should that worry him? The black dot?

Once the sky lightened, he lay back on the bed and fell into a deep, dreamless sleep. When he woke, the night before seemed ridiculous. He felt normal, totally normal.

The shower was working for once. He let the hot water pour over him, raised his face, felt it washing away the night before. He reached for the shower gel.

The water around his feet was stained brown. Then he smelled it – the sharp, metallic smell of blood.

A jolt of fear tugged at the pit of his stomach. He put a hand behind his back and felt the sore, raised wound along his spine.

His head grew muzzy. He crouched down, felt across his hips. Shit! Shit, they'd done it, made him an Elite. He threw up, yellow bitter bile. Once his head cleared, he turned the shower off and dried himself, dabbing at the raw skin on his back. In the mirror he saw paper stitches holding the wound together. He stared at his face. He looked the same, no different. He felt light-headed. His heart was stuttering, but that was fear, terror. Everything else was the same as ever, except for that damned buzzing in his ear.

He sat on the edge of his bed, leaned forwards and covered his face with his hands. Now what? He was a danger to everyone – Pearl, Lucas. It seemed impossible, sitting there in his flat, in broad daylight, that Papa would be able to control him, and yet . . .

He'd keep away from everyone. That's what he'd do. He'd have to hide out, not answer the door.

He messaged Jim, told him he was ill, would be off sick for a while.

His throat ached. He wiped his eyes on his sleeve.

The flat grew chilly. He turned the crappy coal effect fire on, but it was for appearances rather than heat, and made no difference to the temperature of the room. He pulled a heavy wool jumper over his head, but couldn't get warm. Nothing would stop the chills. He lay in bed, clutching a hot water bottle, covered by a duvet and two extra blankets and still he shivered.

His phone buzzed.

Three texts from Pearl. *Spicer, are you all right? Please can you call me?*

Then, a couple of hours later. *Can we at least be friends? I didn't mean to spoil things.*

A new one. *Please don't hate me. I'm so sorry. Lucas needs you. I need you.*

He turned his phone onto silent and cried.

19. PEARL

Sunday dawned bright and frosty – the first really wintry day. Lucas was grouchy, probably picking up on my mood. I could have done without the trip to church, gone without the whole Sunday effort, but it was the only time Lucas got to see the rest of the family, and it was good for him, so I went.

In church, I prayed that God would help me. I prayed that he would protect me from Leo, from Papa, from evil. I prayed that he would forgive me for all the mistakes I'd made. I prayed that none of Art's evil would be passed on to his son. I prayed that I would fall in love with someone good, someone who would be a good father to my child. I prayed that I would find a way to make my parents proud, instead of ashamed – for once.

The ancient church smelled of dust and wood and old bones. The aisle was paved with gravestones, etched with tragic stories, names and dates, Latin inscriptions. Was I walking over bodies? Long decayed bones crumbling, empty eye sockets staring.

After the service, I went into the vestry. 'There's my boy.' Dad crouched down in the vestry doorway and held his arms out wide.

Lucas ran, hurled himself into Dad's embrace.

'Good heavens,' Dad said. 'You'll knock your poor old grandad over.'

Lucas buried his face in Dad's shoulder and I thought how I'd done that as a child. I remembered the rough feel of the wool cassock against my cheek, and I was envious and wished I could be little again, go back to before I made all the wrong decisions, before the world turned dark.

Lucas tilted his head back, looked into Dad's eyes. 'Why don't the worms like church?'

'Don't they?'

Lucas shook his head.

'Well, I expect it's too dry for them,' Dad said, 'because they need moisture, don't they, and earth?'

'No.' Lucas pouted. 'Not *those* worms.'

'Oh, right.' Dad glanced at me. 'Um, well, maybe in case they get trodden on by one of the ladies in their high heels.'

Lucas's frown deepened. 'They can't get trodden on, silly Grandad.'

Dad plonked him back on his feet. 'Go and give your grandma a kiss.' He patted Lucas's head, and Lucas scuttled off to find Mum.

Dad gave me a peck on the cheek. I breathed in the smell of candle wax and incense.

'You look pale,' he said.

'It's the light in here. You should see yourself.'

He laughed, pulled his cassock over his head, and emerged flushed.

'Are there people buried under the aisle?' I said.

'Yes. Why?'

'Nothing.' A shiver rippled over my skin, raised the hairs.

'Are you sure you're all right?' A little worry line appeared between his brows. 'You've lost weight. Are you eating? Do you need money?'

'No, Dad. We're fine. I've just been rushing around, that's all – uni, Lucas. I sometimes forget to eat.'

'Well don't.' He folded his stole – white with gold crosses embroidered at either end – and put it away in the cupboard. 'You have to look after yourself as well, you know.'

'I'm fine. Absolutely fine.' And I was, except for being unbearably lonely, with a huge empty space inside me.

Lydia played football with Lucas in the garden. I watched them and realised I hardly ever played with him, hardly ever heard his contagious laugh which filtered in through the open window.

'She's better than she was,' Dad said. 'Still difficult, of course.'

'Well, she *is* still Lydia.'

'Indeed.'

But she was better with Lucas than I was – more fun, more patient.

Lunch was the usual noisy affair. You'd have thought there were dozens of us there, not just seven. Lydia was the loudest, prattling on about her planned 'gap year'. Every time she mentioned a particularly exotic location, she'd shoot a look at me, as if she thought I'd be envious. She was wasting her time. Being a missionary in some far-flung land had never appealed to me. All that heat, all those flies, all those injections. No thanks.

It finally hit me, after eighteen years of knowing her, that my sister, who I'd always thought of as naughty, rebellious, a nuisance, was a far better person than I was. She would make a better mother, a better friend, an all round better human being. It bothered me. It nagged at me.

Eventually, the conversation moved on to the plaster

peeling behind the altar of Dad's church. Andrew nodded. 'It's almost impossible to get funding. We have to match it, you see. Well!' He lifted his hands in the air. 'Unless there's a miracle and people start coming to church . . .' Everyone made sympathetic noises or tutted.

After that scintillating bit of entertainment, Jim took over. He'd had his teeth done by the look of him – no more green fuzz where they joined the gums. He waffled on about his 'lads' at the station, and how they were struggling to keep up with ever more techno-savvy villains. What the female officers thought of being called lads, he never said. I tried to switch off but Jim's booming voice was hard to ignore.

'. . . out of favour with his boss,' he said. 'So only a matter of time before more . . .' He made speech marks in the air. '. . . *witnesses* crawl out of the woodwork. We could have him for every unsolved murder from here to kingdom come.'

Dad nodded. 'A convenient scapegoat.'

'He's ill, isn't he?' Andrew said.

It was the lack of concern that piqued my interest. Andrew was the kindest, most caring person I knew. It was out of character for him to sound almost glad. Then there was Jim's derisory snort.

'It'll be a trick,' Jim said. 'He's a cunning bastard.'

'Jim.' Mum tilted her head in Lucas's direction.

'Sorry,' Jim said. 'He's such an evil . . .' He exhaled, raised his hands, palms forward.

And with that, the dread started to build, the tightness in my chest, the knotting of my guts. Someone, someone evil, someone they all, even Andrew, hated was ill.

'I've taken the guard off,' Jim went on. 'Protecting tossers like him is not my top priority.'

The chicken in my mouth threatened to choke me.

'I'll be shedding no tears over that bastard,' Jim said. 'He can peg out any time he likes.'

I glanced at Lucas.

'Sorry,' Jim said, mistaking the look.

The lump of chicken sat in my mouth. I tried to swallow but it wasn't going anywhere. A stupid thought popped into my head – that Papa had possessed the chicken, and was going to choke me. I coughed, coughed again, and swallowed, and it went down half way, and lodged there like a stone. But I could speak – just. 'Who's ill?' I aimed for a casual, disinterested tone, and it came off quite well, considering.

'Art.' Andrew said, as if it didn't matter, as if *he* didn't matter. And he smiled – *smiled*.

I had to look away, focus on Lucas, on my boy, but it was like looking at a smaller version of Art. He was alone and ill, and I'd betrayed him with Spicer.

'Is it serious?' I'd never forgive myself. Never.

The conversation had moved on, slipped away from me, and no one heard.

'Is it *serious*?' I said again, loudly this time, interrupting Jim in mid flow.

All eyes on me, everyone frowning, except Lucas, who was stuffing mashed potato and gravy into his mouth, oblivious.

'Sorry?' Mum said.

And I thought, if I say now, she'll wonder, and Mum never missed a trick, and yet to not ask would be torture.

'Art,' I said. 'Art.' I loved his name, loved saying it. 'His illness, is it serious?'

Confusion all round. Jim's face screwed up. 'Who cares?'

'I do,' I said.

'That was a delightful lunch, Maddie,' Andrew said, with a small, polite cough. He placed his knife and fork together on his empty plate, just as he'd been taught to in school, just as all of us did – a signal we were finished.

'For God's *sake*,' I said. 'What's wrong with him?'

Lucas looked up in surprise. Lydia giggled. Everyone else looked baffled.

'Well?' I gripped my cutlery so tightly, the handles cut into my palms. It helped, the pain, helped me to keep from throwing something, from screaming. 'Is he in danger?'

Jim scoffed. 'For f . . .'

'Jim!' Mum said.

'Sorry,' he said. 'Sorry.' He kept blinking, as if he couldn't believe it.

Lucas smiled a wobbly, uncertain smile at everyone in turn.

'He's a human being.' I stood. 'Whatever he's done, none of it was his *fault*.' The last word came out too loudly, almost as a shout.

Jim laughed, spluttered. 'Oh, Christ! Come on, even *you* . .'

I cut him off. 'You have no idea what happened to him. None of you.'

Silence, heavy, laden silence filled the room.

'Can you imagine what he saw?' I said. 'What he was made to do? *Can* you?'

None of them answered. Of course they didn't. They

didn't have a clue. I wanted to leave then, to escape the stares, the shocked faces, the silence, but my limbs wouldn't move.

'He was three years old when they took him.' The words pushed out of my mouth. They kept on coming. I couldn't stop them. 'Three years old. The same age – the same age as . . .' I pointed at Lucas. My hand shook uncontrollably as I realized I was giving myself away. The secret I'd kept so carefully for years was about to be blown open.

Mum was first, of course, as I'd known she'd be. Her eyes stared into mine for a moment. Then she turned to Dad and they held each other's gaze, communicating silently. Dad's gaze slid to Lucas. He closed his eyes.

Jim sat back, mouth open in astonishment. He muttered something under his breath. Probably some profanity or other, because Mum gave him a sharp look.

'He calls Pitt Papa,' I said. 'They all do. Why? Because they think he's their father. They think – they think . . .' My throat closed up. 'They think he loves them.'

'Um . . .' Mum clapped her hands, a fake smile stretching her mouth into a thin line. 'Who'd like coffee?' Her gaze moved from person to person – staccato – manic. 'Tea?' The word sounded desperate, as though everything would be okay, if only everyone would have tea.

'We'll get it.' Dad stood, glanced at me, eyebrows raised. 'Pearl?'

It was his authoritative voice, the one he used so rarely, the one that meant business.

'Of course.' I squeezed Lucas's hand then let it go. I concentrated on putting one foot in front of the other, while my insides did a jig. As I passed Uncle Jim, he shook his head and muttered, 'Unbelievable,' under his breath.

In the kitchen, Dad closed the door behind us, as I knew he would.

My mouth dried up. *Maybe they hadn't realised. Please God, don't let them have realised.*

Dad cleared his throat, stared at the floor. 'Did he force you?'

'God, no.' How could he even *think* that? 'No. He's not . . .' That was what they thought of him? How much they hated him? 'He's not like that – nothing like that.'

'I see.' Those two tight, clipped words encapsulated all his disgust, disappointment, revulsion. He turned his back, took mugs from the cupboard.

My hands shook. The quivering in my stomach made me feel nauseous. Guilt, shame and fear – mostly fear – that Dad wouldn't love me any more, that he would hate me too, and maybe even Lucas, hate us as much as he hated Art.

He filled the kettle. I was aware of time passing, aware of the others, waiting in the next room, no doubt discussing the weather or something equally harmless and safe. The kettle rattled against the tap, played out a rhythm – the rhythm of Dad's pulse.

'What's wrong with him, Dad?'

'Several things.' His tone was flat, emotionless. 'There's evidence of starvation, torture.'

The room tilted around me.

'He's dangerous – deranged, in fact.' Dad let go of the kettle a little too soon. It slammed onto the base.

'Deranged?' Art was always controlled, always calm. 'You mean he's insane?'

'No.' Dad turned to face me. 'He's possessed.'

I laughed. 'That's rubbish. You said yourself. It's mind control.'

He glanced at the door. 'Keep your voice down.'

'It's ridiculous. Papa uses mind games.' I tried to lower my voice. It just got louder. 'That's what you said. You said it.'

He reached out a hand and held my arm. 'Did you *see* Jack at his exorcism. *Did* you? That was more than mind control.'

Memories came flashing back, of Jack's exorcism, of the way his voice wasn't his. That felt like another life, someone else's life, not mine. Definitely not mine. I shook him off, backed away. 'Then why did you say it?'

'Because you weren't well, and . . . we weren't sure, not one hundred percent.' He rubbed at his forehead. 'I'm sorry but I was wrong.'

'Wrong?' I stared at him. '*Wrong?* No.' I needed to think and I couldn't do that with his eyes telling me stuff I didn't want to hear, so I turned my back, steadied myself on the work surface, my hands flat against it, pressed against it, because everything else – my world, my mind, was tipping out of control.

'The thing is, Pearl,' Dad said, 'this affects Lucas.'

'Pardon?' At least I'd remembered my manners. At least there was that.

'Have you noticed any . . ?'

'There's nothing wrong with Lucas.'

He touched my arm, so I had to face him, but I kept my eyes on his hand, because I knew, *knew* his eyes would be probing mine as if I was hiding something.

'Any problems?' Dad said. 'I mean, has he had any – any signs of . . .'

'No!' Too emphatic, almost a shout, because the thought of it was just too horrific to even consider. 'This is ridiculous.'

They were waiting for their tea in the other room. Mum would be making polite conversation, trying to mask the noises from the kitchen. Lydia, she'd be listening, storing up ammunition to use against me later. Well, she had plenty already. What difference would another few secrets make?

'I'll take these in, shall I?' I made it to the other side of the kitchen somehow, haltingly, stiffly. I picked up one of the mugs, and slammed it back down. Tea slopped over the edge and scalded my hand.

'Shit!' I pressed my hand to my side. 'Sorry.'

'Pearl.'

Breathe. Just breathe. In, out, in, out.

'There's nothing wrong with him, Dad.' That was better, less shrill. I had it under control. I put the mugs onto a tray and headed for the door.

Dad opened it. 'Pearl.'

No way. No way was I listening. I smiled as I entered the dining room, registered the curious looks, the shock, and ignored them. 'Here we are.' I placed the tray carefully on the table. 'Sorry about the delay.'

'Are you all right?' Mum said.

'Fine.' My smile felt tight. 'Lucas,' I made my voice sound jolly, 'we need to go home now.'

His brow puckered. 'Don't want to.'

'Come on.' I scooped him into my arms.

He protested, but shut up when I squeezed him hard. We passed Dad in the doorway. 'It won't go away, Pearl,' he said. 'You know that. You know there's only one way.'

'Bye.' I glared at him so hard I thought my eyeballs might pop out.

I was quite proud of the way I drove home – carefully, sticking to the speed limit, giving way to other drivers. I think I even hummed a tune.

20. SPICER

Spicer tried to sleep but hunger gnawed at his stomach. He staggered to the fridge, opened it. Empty except for a half empty bottle of salad cream with dried yellow gunk around the lid. Nothing in the cupboards either. He'd eaten every type of canned food he had until there was nothing left. His stomach growled.

Sweat pumped out of him and yet he couldn't get warm. Food. He'd get some food and then he'd feel okay. He pulled on his jacket, a scarf and gloves and ran to the twenty-four hour supermarket. Too much food, too much choice. He dithered, checked behind him. That fella at the door, the one with the kid, he was watching him for sure. Spicer grabbed a packet of crisps and legged it into the next aisle. A woman pretended to look into the chilled counter. Her eyes slid sideways to him, then away. They had people everywhere, everywhere. Spicer knew that. He knew that.

His mouth dried. He headed for the tills, grabbed stuff as he went – anything he could reach – bread, cereals, chocolate.

The checkout guys – they were all in on it. He could tell by the way they looked away when he caught them watching. Idiots. Did they think he was stupid?

He went to the self-service tills, stood in the queue. Well, they could watch him all they liked. They wouldn't get anything from him. Nothing. Nothing. If only his hands would stop trembling, he'd be okay.

His phone buzzed in his pocket, buzzed like an insect.

He pulled it out, squinted at it.

Tabernacle st. Bring him in alive

The queue hadn't moved. Spicer glanced around. He'd have to come back. They wouldn't wait. Not them.

A woman ran past him, so he followed. He didn't even know why, except that she'd escaped, and so could he.

She ran quickly, but her legs were shorter than Spicer's, and he had to slow his pace in case she clocked him. She stopped at a bus stop, just as the bus drew up. That wasn't right. They hadn't said anything about a bus. He pulled out his phone, checked the text. *Him*, it said, not *her*. He let the woman get on the bus. Tabernacle Street. Now, where the fuck was that?

He typed it into his phone, followed the directions. He slowed his pace as he turned into the street and there was a bloke, shutting the doors on his white van. Thirties, stocky, shaved head.

'Hey,' Spicer shouted.

The man turned. His eyes widened.

'I'm from Mesmeris,' Spicer said. *Go on*, he thought. *Run. Run so I can chase you, so I'll have an excuse to kill you.* His blood jumped at the thought of it, of snuffing him out.

The guy ran. They always did.

So Spicer chased him. That was the way it worked. By the time they reached the end of the road, he'd forgotten why he was chasing this particular guy. It didn't matter. He wanted to play, wanted to hurt someone, wanted someone dead. The rush was incredible. It fired up his body. He felt invincible, powerful. He turned left. His prey had disappeared. Spicer stopped, listened, his heart rate slowing. He sensed him, just the other side of the wall. He could feel him breathing, smell the fear.

He jumped, caught the top of the wall and swung his legs over. And there he was, crouched in the shadows. Spicer laughed. The guy didn't. He wet himself and Spicer tried to recall why he'd hated him in the first place. He looked pathetic, pitiful, crouched like that, his hands covering his head, the steaming pool of urine spreading across the tarmac. There *was* a reason, somewhere, but he couldn't find it and he didn't have time to think. But then he remembered. Papa wanted the man at the house, and he wanted him alive, so he couldn't kill him after all. He felt relief. He didn't want to kill someone like that – someone weak and afraid.

A sharp, stabbing pain in the back of his neck made his vision blur.

He pulled the man to his feet, led him back to the road. It took them a while to reach Spicer's car, then to drive to Papa's, and neither of them said a word. Spicer wasn't sure he'd remember the way, but he did and it was like coming home. Papa was pleased. Even Ruby smiled. 'Nice one.'

Spicer was ecstatic, until Papa sent him away. He wanted to stay there in the family where he belonged. 'I want to watch,' he said. He could barely contain his excitement, the thrill, the fire that shot through his body.

Papa tilted his head to one side. 'Watch what?'

'You kill him.' *Had he said that? Him? Spicer? That wasn't right, was it? That was wrong, to feel like that. That was evil.* His scalp prickled, and stung, as if someone was stabbing at it with a sharp needle. He groaned, lifted a hand to his head and felt things crawling just under the skin, over his skull.

Something fogged his vision. He couldn't see Papa's face clearly any more. It kept moving, sliding out of place. He headed back to his car, his head full of noise – whispers, the low hum of insects, millions of them. He knew what they were doing. They were laying their eggs in the soft, grey matter. He steadied himself against a tree and closed his eyes. The maggots had hatched, that's what had happened. That was why he felt so bad. They were eating his brain, crawling through his skull. He threw up into the undergrowth.

He sat in his car for a while, until he could see straight, then he drove. By the time he drew up outside his home, the buzzing had all but stopped. Inside his head, he knew there lay a decomposing heap of black bodies, wings, spindly legs still twitching. As he put his key in the lock the last one died and all was quiet. They weren't gone though, not them. More eggs sat incubating, nestled deep in the folds of his cortex, waiting.

21. PEARL

I lay low for a few days, stopped answering the phone. Mum left messages, saying how we needed to talk. I didn't want to talk about it. Lucas was Art's son and they'd have to get used to it. It wasn't as if I could change the fact. Since the lunch, they'd felt like the enemy – Jim, Andrew, even Mum and Dad. They all hated the man I loved.

I wanted to see Art for myself, see how ill he really was, whether he was deranged as Dad said. I couldn't imagine it being true. Perhaps they were lying to keep me away from him. I researched online and discovered that prisoners had to request a visit. There was no way of arranging that. Perhaps he didn't even want to see me. I thought he would though, even if only to find out about Lucas. Surely he'd be interested in his son, deranged or not. I tried phoning the nearest prison, but they didn't give out details of their prisoners.

'I'm the mother of his child,' I said.

'I'm sorry.' He didn't sound sorry at all, the bloke on the other end. He sounded dismissive and impatient.

'Well, thank you very much for your help,' I said, as sarcastically as I could. The phone went dead.

'Cheers,' I said. I tried Spicer again. He could get me in there if only he'd talk to me, but he didn't pick up. 'And cheers to you too.'

There had to be a way. I just needed to find it. I made a list, wrote down the facts I knew. First on the list was, *He's ill.* I laughed aloud it was so obvious. Maybe he wasn't in prison at all. If he was as ill as Dad said, he'd be in hospital.

Once I realised that, it was easy to find out where he was. He was listed like any other patient. I phoned saying I was his parish priest. Bingo!

I kept Lucas home from nursery and took him over to my parents early the next morning.

Mum's smile was wary when she opened the door, but she hugged Lucas as tightly as ever and kissed his cheek exactly as she always did. I wanted her to hug *me* like that. I wanted to say sorry, beg for her forgiveness, make her love me again, but I'd hurt her too much this time. She didn't even look me in the eye. It wasn't just the fact that I'd slept with Art, although in her eyes that was 'beyond the pale' as she put it in one of the answerphone messages. It was that I'd lied about Lucas, made them think he was something he wasn't – Spicer's child.

She stepped aside. 'Come in.'

I wore my guilt like a coat, but it was one I was used to wearing – old and worn and shabby, and it fitted me perfectly.

'He's a bit off colour.' I kept my voice light, relaxed, as if I hadn't noticed the chill in her voice, her eyes, her everything. 'Do you think you could look after him for an hour or so?'

'Did you get my calls?' The corners of her mouth were tight, downturned.

I didn't want to see her sadness, didn't want to feel that sharp stab in my heart. I pretended not to hear her question. 'I just need to do a bit of shopping before town gets busy. You know how grumpy Lucas gets.' Lies and more lies. 'Do you mind if I nip to the loo?'

She nodded. 'Listen, we need to have a proper talk.'

'Not now, Mum. When I get back, okay? We'll talk about it then.' I smiled, focussing on her eyebrows, not her eyes.

'Right.'

'Grandma.' Lucas called her on cue to help him reach a jigsaw puzzle.

I ran upstairs to the bathroom, turned the tap on, then slipped into Mum and Dad's bedroom. Mum's uniforms hung together in the wardrobe. I slipped one from the hanger and folded it into my bag. Hopefully I wouldn't need her pass. If I did . . . well, I'd deal with that if it happened. I dashed into the bathroom, flushed the loo and washed my hands. She'd hear every sound, I knew.

When I came downstairs, she was standing at the bottom. My heart did a little flip.

She lowered her voice to a whisper, nodded pointedly towards Lucas. 'He's not himself.'

'He's fine.' I didn't have time to think about it. I gave her a peck on the cheek, tried not to notice the way she shrank from me. 'He gets tired, that's all. Stop worrying.'

She said something else, but I talked over her. 'Thanks so much. I won't be long.'

I flashed a smile at her pinched face. There wasn't time to reassure her. I'd do that later, when Art was safe.

I'd managed to miss the morning rush hour – just, so the traffic wasn't too heavy. My biggest problem was going to be CCTV, so I stopped off on the way and bought a pair of cheap reading glasses from a pound shop and a pale blue scarf, which I wrapped around my head until it vaguely resembled a hijab.

It was a doddle getting onto the ward dressed in Mum's

uniform. Other staff even said hello to me. I stopped a porter pushing an empty wheelchair. 'Could you tell me where Andreas Todd is, please?'

'In a side ward, on his own.' He pointed at a door to the side of the main ward. 'Just as well too.'

'Thank you.' I stared at the door for a good minute after he left. My courage deserted me. My dream of rescuing Art had been just that – a dream, a fantasy. Not for a moment had I really imagined being able to do it, not really. I hadn't even thought it through. My heart banged so hard it made my neck, even my ears hurt. He was there, behind that door. A few paces away from me. The love of my life. And Papa was going to use him as a scapegoat if I didn't do something to stop it. This was about saving him from a lifetime in prison for someone else's crimes. I couldn't just walk away.

The door stood ajar. I pushed at it, stepped inside, raised my eyes.

His skin was papery white – actually white, the colour of the sheets. He lay on his back, his mouth slightly open, asleep. Cavernous face, hollow cheeks, shadowed eyes. Thin, so thin. The blue of his eyes showed through the transparent lids. He looked like a boy, not a man. A boy – starved and vulnerable and beaten. His tousled black hair stood out against the pillow. His arms lay on top of the covers. A drip fed into his left wrist.

My chest was tight, so tight I couldn't breathe. I wanted to run away. I wanted to hold him in my arms. I wanted to cry, to laugh, to scream. I did nothing.

His lips parted slightly every time he breathed out. I stood there watching his beauty, drinking it in like a sponge, having been starved of that face for so long. His eyelids flickered. A dream. I wondered what he saw in his head. Had he ever dreamed of me? He shifted position, frowned, made a small noise, a groan of pain and I started forward. Instinct, to want to comfort him. He rolled onto his side and his eyes opened, looked straight into mine.

'What the . . ?' He tried to sit up.

'Don't.' I ran to him, held his shoulders. 'Don't. You'll hurt yourself.' I hugged him then, wrapped my arms around him and held him close. And I cried, cried because I could never tell him what I'd done, because I'd have to live with the guilt forever. Tears poured out, soaked into his hospital gown. For ages, it seemed, we stayed like that. He had no choice, of course, held captive by his blankets, the drip, my arms.

'You have to come . . .' A small sob escaped. 'Come home with me.'

'Why?'

I released my grip a little, so I could see his face. It was like looking at Lucas – a bigger, rougher version, an adult version.

'They're blaming you for everything,' I said. 'They're going to lock you up.'

'Surprise, surprise.' A bitter smile.

'Leo tried to snatch our baby.'

His eyes narrowed. 'When was that?'

'The week before last.'

He threw the bedcovers off.

'What are you doing?' I tried to hold onto him.

He shook me off, yanked the drip out. Blood spurted over the white sheets. His pale face went grey. He swung his legs off the bed, pressing the heel of his hand onto the wound. A tray stood on a trolley by the door. I tore open a dressing and wrapped it around his wrist to stem the bleeding.

'My clothes.' He pointed at the bedside cabinet.

I ran to the door and closed it properly, then took his clothes from the cupboard. I hugged them. They smelled of him, and I loved him. I loved him.

He took them from me. 'Where's the child now?'

'With my parents.' I ignored 'the child'. He didn't know Lucas – not yet. He wouldn't see him like that when he did. I kept glancing at the door. Doctors did their rounds in the mornings, didn't they? If anyone came in . . .

'Can you . . ?' He pointed at the back of his hospital gown.

I untied it. Bones jutted from his shoulders, his hips. Scars and weals covered his back, crossing and re-crossing his 'mark'. He turned to pick up his jumper. Black and yellow bruises stained his sides and belly.

'Who did that?'

He looked away.

'*Papa?*' I pulled his arm, turned him to face me. 'Papa did that to you?'

His set jaw, mouth clamped shut, said it all.

'Why?'

He shrugged. 'Who knows? Bored, maybe.'

Bored? He'd been tortured because Papa was *bored?* A wave of tenderness made me catch my breath. How thin he was, wasted away. Matted hair, scarred scalp.

'I'll look after you.' I helped him on with his clothes, flinching in sympathy as each new scar, wound or bruise was uncovered. 'Damn that pig of a man,' I said, my teeth clamped together. 'Damn him. He is *never* coming near you again – not ever.'

Art laughed. At least, it sounded like a laugh although his face showed nothing, not even a hint of a smile.

No one tried to stop us as we left the hospital. His arm across my shoulders, I supported him through the corridors and across the car park. A watery sun threatened to break through the light cloud, but the air was chilly and felt damp against my skin. I was worried he'd catch a chill, even with a jacket on, being so thin. He winced as he lowered himself into the passenger seat. He leaned his head back against the headrest and closed his eyes.

For a moment, I thought he'd died. I'd never seen anyone look so ill before. 'Are you all right?'

He groaned. '*All right* may be pushing it a bit.'

I started the engine, turned the heating on full and prayed silently all the way home. *Please, please God, don't let him die. Not now. Not now.*

I helped him up the stairs and into my bed. I filled a hot water bottle and tucked the duvet around him. 'You have to stay up here,' I said. 'We'll decide what to do when you're better.'

'Better?'

'When you're well.'

'Right.' He nodded. 'Okay, but I need to see Spicer.'

'When you're well.' I drew the curtains, went downstairs and made him a cup of tea. By the time I got back, he was asleep. Fast asleep. I watched him and thought how I'd longed for this, to have him there with me. It didn't matter that it couldn't last. I was happy with that, just that, being able to see him, talk to him, hug him.

At lunchtime, I made him soup. He sat up and I fluffed the pillows behind him, the way Mum had always done when I was ill as a child. He watched me, his lip twitching.

'What?' I said.

'Nothing.'

I went downstairs, washed and tumble-dried Mum's uniform, then tried to do some work. It was impossible to concentrate. I turned on daytime TV and flicked through the channels: a crap quiz show with canned laughter, a cookery demonstration, someone doing up a house. The images stopped registering as one clip followed another. I sat up, ready to switch off, when Art's face appeared.

The wind ruffled his black hair. He squinted into the sunshine. This was old film, taken outside Papa's house in late springtime, when the acid green leaves had already unfurled and the air would have been warm and scented with lilac.

He looked so beautiful – the blue of his eyes brought out by the navy shirt he wore, collar unbuttoned. I didn't ever remember seeing him in a shirt. It must have been for the press, to give a professional appearance, a veneer of respectability. No one gazing into those clear eyes, watching that delicious mouth, hearing that smooth, soft voice, could ever doubt him.

The voice-over said something about Brighton, about murders and young people. The fog in my head meant I didn't catch it. Perhaps I didn't want to.

And then, before I could press the off button, the picture changed to a studio and Papa appeared. He stared out of the screen as if he was looking at me alone. He brushed back his snow-white hair and smiled. A mocking smile, superior, arrogant. He sat in a black armchair, relaxed and confident in his charcoal designer suit and lilac silk tie. A well-groomed, middle-aged man with white hair and black eyebrows. Nothing to say how evil he was, except perhaps the eyes and the slack, weak mouth.

'You bastard,' I muttered. 'You murdering bastard.'

The camera panned out to show a jug of water and two glasses on a low table, then a woman, sitting opposite Papa in an identical chair. She must have been in her late thirties, early forties. The dyed, blue-black hair, the severe bob and thick, blunt fringe did nothing for her – made her look tired and old. Did she have any idea how scary Papa was? I doubted it.

She held a few sheets of paper in her left hand and pulled at the hem of her pink tweed skirt with the right. It was a nice skirt, but too short. She sat with her knees together, facing right, then left, then right again, as though she couldn't decide which leg looked best. I concentrated on the details. It stopped me thinking.

'Mr Pitt,' she began.

'Howard, Maxine,' Papa said, with a sleazy smile, 'please.'

'Howard.' Her cheeks flushed, the stupid woman. 'Andreas Todd is a prominent member of . . .'

Papa held up a hand and stopped her. '*Was. Was* a prominent member. He no longer has any association with our religion – none.' He gazed into the camera. 'My thanks go to the brave witnesses who came forward and named this shameful coward.'

I choked on my saliva. Papa calling Art a coward?

'These terrible acts of violence,' Papa said, 'have brought

shame on our faith.' He cleared his throat, and closed his eyes. 'My heart breaks for the grieving families of those tragic young people.'

A picture flashed into my head of Papa, the real Papa – eyelids drooping, slack lips glistening. 'Beautiful violence,' he'd said, his low, breathy voice right in my ear. 'Inflicting pain on another is . . . true beauty.'

My stomach heaved. Art hadn't killed those kids in Brighton. He'd been the other end of the country. I knew that, and I was going to have to tell the police, tell them I was there, that I'd seen them, the kids, that I'd lied. Perjury. I'd go to prison, and Lucas . . .

Maxine crossed her legs, took a sip of water. 'You've taken a number of young people into your care over the years. Is that correct?'

'Correct, yes.'

'They could be classed as, perhaps, problem children?'

'Indeed.' Papa nodded. 'Indeed, yes – problem children.'

'Some are asking . . .' Maxine fidgeted. Not surprising, the way Papa was staring at her. 'Some are asking if it was wise to allow – vulnerable children to be fostered by a movement such as Mesmeris.'

'Really?' Papa frowned. 'Are they? Isn't it the task of a religious organisation to offer a shelter to those in need, those on the margins of society?'

'Um . . .'

'These children were given the best education, healthcare. They have been fed and clothed to the highest standards.' He lowered his voice and leaned forwards, as if it were a private conversation between the two of them. 'Most of all, Maxine,' he smiled, 'we provided – dare I say, a family.'

Maxine's cheeks flamed, her eyes sparkled. 'And – Mr Todd?'

'Ah.' Papa shook his head. His mouth turned down. 'I'm afraid Andreas must have been corrupted by others outside our faith.'

Maxine glanced down at her notes. 'Is it true your followers see you as a god?'

'A *god?*' Papa's chuckle was humble, embarrassed. He sat back, opened his hands, palms up. 'Maxine. More a father figure, surely.'

'Not a dictator then, as some have suggested?' She laughed nervously.

Papa pursed his lips, and frowned. 'It's true I give my children boundaries, a framework.' He formed a square with his hands. 'It makes them feel secure, Maxine, and when children feel secure, they are happy. Too many children are raised without discipline, don't you agree?'

Maxine nodded.

Papa leaned forwards, and stared into Maxine's eyes. 'Everyone needs discipline, Maxine – even you.'

They stared, unblinking, into each other's eyes. One second passed, two. Papa's lips stretched into a slow smile.

Someone coughed in the background. Maxine started. 'Yes, well,' she said, flustered. 'Um . . . thank you.' She cleared her throat. 'Howard Pitt there, charismatic, er, leader of Mesmeris.'

'If I may say one thing?' Papa's black eyes stared intently into the camera. 'Nothing, I know, will bring these young people back, but I want to make something *absolutely* clear. The actions of this one,' he pointed at the camera, 'rogue member go against *everything* Mesmeris stands for – obedience, discipline, justice.'

I laughed, laughed until I couldn't breathe, until the laughter turned to tears, until I thought I might be sick. Then I turned the television off, picked up my coat and car keys, and left the house.

22. PEARL

When I got to my parents' house, Lucas was in Lydia's room. She was reading him The Wind in the Willows. He looked so happy there, sitting next to her on the bed. I made him nervous, frightened even. There he felt safe. Poor boy, I thought, having me as a mother. I managed to sneak Mum's uniform back into her wardrobe. It didn't look as pristine as the other one. Hopefully she wouldn't notice.

Lucas didn't want to leave. Lydia bribed him into going downstairs with the promise of a banana. I waited impatiently while he ate it, then he wailed and stiffened in my arms when I tried to pick him up.

'For God's *sake*,' I said.

Dad came through the front door. 'Ah, saw your car.'

'We're just . . .' I pointed at the door.

'We need to talk,' Dad said.

'I have to get back, Dad.'

'About the worms in Lucas's head,' Dad said – in front of Lucas, as if the bloody things existed.

'Grandad's going to take them out,' Lucas said. 'Grandad knows all about worms.'

'Does he now?'

Mum took Lucas from my arms, her mouth a thin, determined line.

I felt ambushed, outmanoeuvred. Dad motioned towards his study. Of course, I did as I was told. What else could I do?

'It's simple.' Dad's smile looked ridiculous, as if he'd

drawn it on his pale, worried face. 'Nothing like . . .'

'Like Jack?' I stood, clenched my fists over and over to get my circulation going. 'Not all that vomiting then,' I said, my voice high and loud, 'and pain, and agony and all that *shit*.' I was back in that church, that night. I could smell it – *smell* it – blood and sulphur and sick and death.

'It would be nothing like . . .'

'No,' I said. 'Nothing like it. A doddle.'

'It's . . .' He looked weary, careworn. 'He's done nothing. He's an innocent.'

'Yes. He is. He *is*. So he doesn't need . . .' Something was in the room with us. Hovering just above the floor – a layer of mist or fog, but dark. I blinked but it didn't go away. It rose up behind Dad like a tidal wave, growing darker and thicker, black and glossy. He didn't see it coming. Why didn't he see it? Hear it? It was so loud, so dark, and there he was, still talking, talking, his mouth going yak, yak, yak, the words swallowed up by the roar of the wave. I tried to warn him, waved my arms, but it was too late. It washed over him until there was just a wall of glossy blackness and, in the middle, there was his mouth, still at it, forming words I'd never hear, and then that too was gone. The wave came towards me, covering everything in its path, Dad, the desk, the carpet – closer and closer it came. I could hear it breathing. I had to get out and warn Mum, warn Lucas. Already the wave was overshadowing me. It loomed over my head and at the top – way, way up, was a white crest where it curled, hesitated, quivered. I stood, felt the chair fall, heard it clatter as it hit the floor, even there, in the hollow of the wave. I turned to where the door should have been but there was only sand

and grass and, beyond that, the sea, so I ran toward it, over the hillocks, through the needle-sharp Marram grass. I tried to scream, but no noise came out of my mouth. Roaring filled my head, my ears. I tripped, fell flat, my face in the gritty sand. I started digging with my hands. I could hide in the sand and no one would ever find me. I dug and dug, down, down, until daylight disappeared and all was sand, all around me, pressing on me until I couldn't move forward or backwards. It was so dark, and I couldn't remember how to get back to the surface, couldn't remember which way was up. The sand was in my eyes, covering my nose and mouth so I couldn't breathe.

I woke in my old bed. Mum stood beside me. She placed a cup down on the bedside table. It was light outside. Birdsong filtered through the window. I sat up, confused. It was as if time had gone back years to when I was young and happy.

'The doctor sedated you,' Mum said.

So time hadn't gone back then. I was still me, still crazy. 'Why?'

'You got a bit – upset. You . . .' She cleared her throat. 'You were trying to claw your way through the wall.'

I'd remember that. Surely even *I'd* remember something like that.

She turned her back on me and tilted her head back, as if she'd seen something fascinating on the ceiling. There was nothing fascinating up there though, not even a cobweb.

'You tore your nails, Pearl.'

I checked. Of course I did, and she was right, naturally. My fingertips were scratched and sore, the nails shredded.

She turned to face me, her eyes shiny, red-rimmed. 'We

had to call him. We were afraid you'd hurt yourself.'

'Yes,' I said. 'I'm sorry. Sorry, I don't remember.' My mind was a blank. The last thing I remembered was the black tidal wave . . .

I swung my legs out of bed. 'How long have I been asleep?' It couldn't have been long. It was still light outside.

She glanced at her watch. 'It's ten past nine now so . . .'

'Ten past *nine*?' I checked out of the window. 'And it's still light?'

Mum frowned. 'In the morning.'

'*Morning*? You mean it's *Thursday*?' I stood. Art was on his own, with no one to look after him. 'I have to go.' I avoided her hands as she reached out to grab me, to stop me.

'Don't be silly,' she said.

I didn't want to worry her, make her afraid for me, for Lucas, but Art – Art was relying on me and I was all he had. *All* he had. I pushed my feet into my Doc Martens.

'You're not well enough, Pearl.'

'I'm fine.' I grabbed my Parka, shoved my arms into the sleeves.

'Move back home for a while. At least until . . .'

I zipped up my coat.

Mum caught my arm. 'You'll not be wanting to go back to hospital, will you?' An implied threat. No, not implied – overt, obvious, terrifying.

They thought I was insane again. They thought the thing, the tidal wave wasn't real. They thought . . .

'I have to go home.' He could die of thirst. He could be dead already, in my bed, alone. I shook Mum off and opened the bedroom door. 'I'm sorry, Mum, but I have to.'

Short of physically restraining me, there was nothing she could do. I ran down the stairs, was in such a panic that Mum's words were just a garbled noise in my head.

'Lucas,' I shouted. All was quiet – too quiet. 'Where is he?' They'd taken him – taken my boy.

'Your dad took him to nursery.' Mum clung on to the stair rail, her face pale and drawn. 'We thought it best to stick to routine.'

'Yes.' That made sense. That made perfect sense. They wouldn't take him from me, not Mum and Dad. Not them.

'Children feel secure if . . .'

She sounded like Papa. 'Yes, yes,' I said to shut her up because I didn't want to think about Papa, or worms or exorcisms or any of that stuff because then that tidal wave would come back and I'd never get to Art. I pulled the front door open.

'You can't drive,' she said. 'The sedation . . .' She was going to make a grab for me. I could see it in her eyes, in the set of her mouth – that determined look she got when nothing would stop her.

I ran, ran down the path and out to my car.

'Pearl.' She was running after me. I could hear her feet pounding down the path, but I was faster. I hurled myself into the car, slammed the door and locked it. She shouted something, but I couldn't hear it over the engine. I drove away and didn't look back.

I sped home and all the way, images of a dehydrated, emaciated Art flashed into my head. I imagined him on the floor of the bedroom, collapsed, a hand stretched out towards the door. I imagined him calling for help, and no one hearing. I put the key in the door, held my breath, and pushed it open.

The house was silent. 'Art?' *Please, please be alive.*

A figure moved from the shadows in the living room. I caught my breath. He stood, silhouetted against the window. I couldn't take my eyes off him. Every pore. I loved every pore, every molecule, every atom of him. I pushed the door shut with my heel.

He took one step towards me. Then another – slow, panther-like, stalking his prey. Every part of my body was on fire. I could barely breathe. My heightened senses noticed everything – the scar on his right hand, across the knuckles, the soft, hushed padding of his crepe-soled shoes, the way his t-shirt moved across his torso as he moved. I felt him breathing, his mouth slightly open. I noticed the scar above his left eyebrow – white, ancient – and the other, newer one, red and swollen on his cheekbone. I watched him swallow, watched his long legs cover the distance between us. I felt his heat, smelled his skin, heard his heartbeat matching my own.

His kiss, rough, brutal, scratched my skin. His lips bruised mine. Rough hands felt like sandpaper on my skin. He held me so tightly, it made me lightheaded. Years. Years I'd waited.

His mouth covered mine and I was lost, lost in the frantic, desperate need for him.

Afterwards, we lay tangled together on the sofa. I caught his hands. He had the most beautiful hands – masculine, but beautiful. Long fingers and . . .

Where his short, clean nails had been, there was ugly scarred skin.

'What happened to your hands?'

He looked away. 'Nothing.'

'He pulled your nails?'

His Adam's apple moved as he swallowed.

'I hate him.' I kissed his hands, his poor, scarred fingertips. 'I hate him so much.' He lifted my chin and kissed me, more gently this time, slipping his tongue into my mouth, and it started all over again. I felt I'd never have enough of him – never.

I traced a line down his chest, kissed his warm skin. I touched the scars and bruises, some old, long-healed, some fresh, vivid, violent. I ran my fingertips over them as if that would heal them, make them disappear, as if they'd never happened.

He sat up, his back to me. How I detested that scar carved into his skin, down his spine and across his hips. The mark of Mesmeris, of evil, of Papa.

'Lucas says there are worms in his head.' I touched Art's matted hair. 'It makes me think of you.'

He turned his head to look at me. His eyes were so dark. I didn't like the way he stared, unblinking.

'What is it?' I said.

'Has he been bitten? Insect bite, sting – something like that?'

'No. No. Is that how it . . ?'

'Any broken skin?'

My stomach tightened, just a notch. 'A scratch, that's all, grazed knees, things like that.'

'Kids are always . . .'

'Yes -- yes.' Of course kids always had scratches, bumps and bruises. They ran too fast, they fell over.

He pulled his t-shirt on over his head. 'What kind of

scratch?'

The knot in my stomach grew so tight it was painful. 'He slipped off his chair in nursery.'

He nodded. 'So you weren't there?'

'No.' I should have been there, should have protected him.

'Where is it? The scratch?'

I pointed to the small of my back, afraid, so afraid.

'I'll need to see it.'

Yes, yes he needed to see it. Just a scratch, that was all.

'And I need to see Spicer,' he said. 'It's urgent. I want you to get him here.'

The thought of them together made me feel ill. Would they know? Know what I'd done? It was more likely that Art would. He was better at reading people. He'd know, and then . . .

'Get him here – today.' A note of impatience crept into his voice.

'We don't talk any more, me and Spicer.'

'Why not?' His eyes narrowed.

'No reason.' I couldn't look at him. His eyes were too sharp, too perceptive. Instead, I got off the sofa and pulled my clothes on, brushed my hair. 'I'll ask him.'

I could feel his eyes watching me, accusing me. At least I thought I could, but when I turned around he had his head back, eyes closed.

23. PEARL

I went around to Spicer's place. For the first time, the communal front door was locked. I rang the bell, heard it clanging in the hallway.

The door opened and a girl with greasy, lank hair came through backwards, pulling a baby's buggy behind her.

I helped, held the door.

'Ta,' she said. She smelled of chip fat and fags.

I went into the narrow passageway, traipsed up the two flights of stairs to Spicer's room and knocked.

'What?' He sounded groggy.

'It's me.' My face flamed. My whole body flamed.

Silence.

'Can I come in?'

'No.' Perhaps he had a girl in there.

'I have a message for you, that's all. Don't worry. I have no intention of repeating my mistake.'

He made a noise like a cough, or a hiccough, or maybe a laugh. Maybe he was laughing at me, the desperate shag from a one-night stand.

'You're acting like a child, for God's sake,' I said.

I waited.

Nothing.

'What about Lucas? Are you dumping him as well?'

Movement from inside the room, and finally the door opened. I was all ready to have a go at him. I wanted to punch him, but when I saw his face, my anger drained away.

His skin was pasty, clammy. His eyes red-rimmed. The

curtains were drawn in the flat, the fire on. The heat was almost unbearable.

'It's like an oven in here.' I pushed past him, turned the fire off, pulled the curtains and opened the window. He looked even worse in daylight. 'What's the matter?'

'Nothing.' His eyes were shadowed, dull, his face thinner than before. He hadn't shaved, and by the smell of him, hadn't washed either. The Greek god I'd had in my bed just over a week before had disappeared without trace, as if he had never existed.

I went to feel his forehead, but he backed away, lifted an arm to protect himself, as if he was frightened of me.

'Spicer, you're ill.' I moved my head to get in his eye line, held his gaze while I touched the back of my hand to his forehead. It was cool. No fever. 'Let's get you some fresh air, shall we?' The heat in the room was making me feel faint. 'We'll go for coffee. I'll buy.'

His eyes seemed larger, sunk as they were in the sockets, but he let me lead him downstairs and outside. Where had my Spicer gone, the one I relied on, the strong, sensible, grounded one?

It wasn't far to the coffee shop. I slipped my arm through his and we walked in awkward silence. Perhaps he'd been ill all that time. Maybe that was why he hadn't come over, hadn't called. Whatever it was must have come on suddenly. Now I felt guilty about him too – about not checking on him, making sure he was all right.

He barely looked up as I set the coffees on the table. The way he fidgeted, kept glancing at the door, made me nervous, as if I wasn't already in enough of a state. Where to start? Maybe it wasn't a good idea to mention Art when he looked so ill. Then I remembered how insistent Art had been.

Spicer stirred his coffee with a shaking hand, erasing the heart-shaped latte art. His nails were bitten, shredded. He winced, shook his head. 'Is there something in my hair?'

'No.'

'There's buzzing.' He lowered his head, shook like a dog again.

'Let me have a look.' I stood, went to his side and examined his fair head – so fair that nothing would be able to hide in it. As my hand went through his hair, I felt a surge of tenderness that made me want to hug him, make everything better. 'It's fine,' I said. 'There's nothing.'

He caught my hand. 'You know I love you, don't you? You're the only family I have – you and Lucas.' His grip tightened until it hurt.

'I know.' And I did. I kissed the top of his head, because he was my soul mate – my mixed up, messed up soul mate.

I sat back in my seat and took a deep breath. 'Art wants to see you.'

No reaction. He played with his spoon, spinning it on the table.

'He's at my house,' I said.

Still no reaction. He seemed to have switched off. The spoon went round and round, round and round.

'Will you come back with me?'

'No.' The spoon skittered off the table and clattered to the floor. He made no attempt to pick it up, just stared at the spot where it had been, as if wondering where it had gone.

'He's ill, Spicer. He needs you.'

He flung his head back and laughed. I jumped right off my chair. It sounded so out of place, so harsh. Every head in the place turned and stared.

'Stop it.' I caught his hand.

'What?' His eyes were blank, empty. He was out of it – completely off his head.

'What've you taken?'

'Nothing.' He sat hunched over his coffee, mouth turned down. A teardrop ran down his cheek, hung on his chin, then plopped onto the table. The small dark spot spread, made my heart hurt.

'Spicer, what is it?'

He shrugged. 'Stuff going on.'

'What stuff?'

His lips thinned, whitened. 'None of your *business.*' The sudden change in tone from the Spicer I knew to a hate-filled stranger took my breath away. Darkness emanated from him in waves. The whole world had gone crazy. Spicer, my rock, had become quicksand, unpredictable, dangerous. He caught my wrist and squeezed it hard, his bones against my bones. 'He's a wanker.' His eyes stared into mine. The pupils were huge, black. 'He doesn't give a *shit* about you or Lucas. Get him out of your house. Out of your . . .' He shook his head. 'Out of your *bed.*' His body juddered – the vibration ran all the way up my arm, as if an electric current ran through him. 'Just . . . get him out.' He twitched, blinked. 'Shit.'

He knew. He knew.

'You're hurting me,' I said.

He released my wrist, turned his face away. No apology. Nothing.

'I have to go now,' I said.

He half-laughed, nodded. 'Yeah, you don't want to keep him waiting.'

'See a doctor, Spicer.'

He stared at his cold coffee. I don't even know if he heard me.

I left him there, sitting with his demons, while I went home with my own, *to* my own.

24. PEARL

Lucas had a good day at nursery. His sunny smile made me smile, even though everything was such a mess – everything but him. We stopped off at the supermarket to get some food, tins of soup for Art, ice cream for Lucas – as if buying him a treat would make up for everything, put it right. The queues were long. As we drew nearer the till, the racks of magazines and sweets on either side of us, a headline caught my eye. *Manhunt.* For a moment, I thought he was really there – Art. Except there were several of him – eight, maybe nine – mostly the same picture. A still from the TV footage of the previous night perhaps. Same blue shirt. His black hair windswept, the sun on his angular cheekbones. His eyes, even there, in crap images on cheap newspaper – even there, they burned.

It was front-page news. His face, his beautiful face, stared out under lurid headlines – *Cop killer,* with one, two, sometimes three exclamation marks – *Sick cult psycho, Pervert, Svengali.* Perhaps some of it was true – or all of it.

'Mummy.' Lucas said.

'Yes.' I couldn't take my eyes off the papers.

'Mummy.' Insistent now.

'Yes, just . . .'

'You're next, love.' The woman behind me tapped my arm.

'Sorry.' I lifted my shopping out of the basket onto the conveyor belt.

'Disgustin', innit?' the woman said, one over-plucked eyebrow raised, one lowered.

'Mmm.'

She shook her head. 'Human sacrifices, they say. That's sick, that is.'

I wanted to put my hand over her mouth to shut her up.

'Poor families,' the checkout girl said. 'That's what I think.'

Families. They had families. They were someone's children, and they were dead, because . . .

'He's a nutter.' She nodded at the papers. 'That's what they say.'

I handed the cash over with shaking hands.

The woman behind me nodded, mouth pursed. 'Can't believe they let 'im go.' She shook her head. 'Bloody criminal, that's what it is.'

She glanced down at Lucas, then to the paper and back again.

I pulled Lucas close, shielded him from her view. 'Don't believe everything you read in the papers.' I snapped my bag shut and walked out.

The papers weren't lying though – not completely. I wished they were, but they weren't. A killer, a sadist, was asleep in my bed.

When we got back, I sat Lucas in front of the TV, volume up, and gave him an ice cream.

Art was sitting up in bed. He looked better, a lot better than Spicer had.

'You're in the papers,' I said.

'Am I?'

'Front page news.' I held my hands up to show the size of the headline. 'Cop killer.'

He snorted.

'Sick psycho. Svengali.'

'Don't mind the Svengali bit.' His lips twitched.

'Have you killed a copper?'

He shrugged. 'Probably – at some point.'

Probably, as if it was something that would slip his mind, like an item on a shopping list.

'They love a bit of drama, the papers,' he said. 'Always exaggerating.'

'*Are* they exaggerating?'

He stared, unblinking. 'No.' He looked so sad, it broke my heart.

'It's not your fault, the stuff you've done.'

A ghost of a smile crossed his lips.

'It's Papa. He made you like that.'

He nodded – one small nod. 'You think I'd be different – without him?'

'Definitely.'

'I wouldn't enjoy inflicting pain?'

'No.'

'I'm not sure you're right,' he said, but I thought I saw a glimmer of hope in his eyes, a desire to be different, better, but then it was gone and I couldn't be sure it had been there at all. 'Did you see Spicer?' he said, after a moment.

'Yes.' I rubbed my wrist, could see the red imprints of Spicer's fingertips. They would turn to blue bruises, I knew. I covered them with my hand, in case Art saw them. 'He's not well.'

'What kind of not well?'

I shrugged. 'A virus probably. I don't know.'

'His hair?'

'What?'

'His hair – has he torn it.'

'He's not *you*, Art. He's nothing like you.'

A small smile. 'You haven't seen him in action.'

I turned away, collected the dirty cups together.

'He likes the chase,' Art said.

I paused.

'Pursuit's his thing. Once he's caught them, he loses interest, walks away.'

He wasn't talking about me and yet it felt as if he was.

'He likes to think he's a good guy, but he's no better than the rest of us.'

'You're wrong.' I don't know why I said it. Because it annoyed me, I suppose, him comparing Spicer to Mesmeris, to murderers, torturers. But I shouldn't have said it because Art's lip twitched. 'Ah,' he said.

'What?'

'Have you slept with him?'

'Of course not.' I should have said it was none of his business. That's what I should have said, but it was too late now. At least I remembered not to look away, remembered not to look down. I stared back and hoped he couldn't see the vein pounding in my neck.

He stared for a long time, as if he was searching inside my head. I thought I should probably say something, act as if it was nonsense, but I didn't. I couldn't move. Eventually, he looked away, released me. His eyelids closed. 'I'm tired.'

I left him to sleep, went downstairs and concentrated on Lucas. Once I'd put him to bed, read him a story, and made sure he was asleep, I shook Art awake.

His eyelids opened slowly, as if it was a huge effort.

'You said you needed to see it,' I said. 'The scratch.'

He nodded. I told him to wait on the landing. Lucas stirred as his bedroom light came on but didn't open his eyes. He lay on his front, his right arm over his head. I lifted the back of his pyjama top as gently as I could. He murmured, shoved his thumb in his mouth and sucked on it.

Art hovered by the door, shifting his balance from foot to foot. I'd never seen him fidget before.

Once the scratch was visible, I waved Art in. He was so light on his feet, silent as a ghost. It made the hairs on my arms stand up, the way he moved across the room. I pointed at the scratch. It was so tiny I felt ridiculous for even mentioning it. He'd laugh, surely, except Art never laughed. Never. He'd roll his eyes then, or groan, think me crazy, a neurotic mother.

No rolled eyes. Nothing. He straightened up and walked out.

I tucked Lucas back under the covers too roughly, hurrying. He woke and wrapped his arms around my neck. It seemed ages before I could get him to let go and go back to sleep.

It was tiny. A tiny scratch. Laughable really. Still, my pulse hurt as I left the room.

Art hadn't gone back to bed. He was right outside the room, his back pressed against the wall, his head back, staring at the ceiling.

'Well?' I whispered.

He didn't need words. He just looked at me with those eyes.

I shook my head. A pointless, useless gesture. 'He's *not*

infected,' I said. 'He can't be. That's not possible. Papa's just a man. A vile one, a sick one, but he's not a god.'

'No.' He agreed. He said it.

'He doesn't have powers.' I meant it as a statement, but it sounded like a question – no, not a question, a plea. 'He can't control . . .' I remembered Art tearing his hair out, convinced there were maggots in his head. Maggots, worms, worms, maggots.

'It's mind control,' I said, my voice tiny.

He headed downstairs so I followed him.

'What do we do?'

He lifted his jacket from the back of the chair.

'You can't leave us,' I hissed.

The jacket was on. His shoes were on his feet. He bent to tie the laces.

'You can't leave me with this.'

But he *was* leaving. He'd turned his back already.

'Art.'

He was almost at the door. I ran after him. 'Don't you dare walk away.' I yanked his arm, punched his chest. 'Don't you *dare*.'

He caught my hands, held my wrists. Hard eyes.

'You're afraid,' I said, although it was me who was trembling, not him.

He half-laughed, shook his head and released me, then opened the door.

'You're terrified you might feel something for him,' I said to his back. 'For your child.'

I'd gone too far, had forgotten how threatening he could be. His fists clenched at his sides, the knuckles white, and for a moment, I thought he might turn and hit me but he didn't. He walked out without a word.

I kicked the door shut. He was never going to let us in – me and Lucas. He was incapable of love. He couldn't risk it, the pain, and there was only one person to blame for that – Papa.

25. SPICER

Spicer paced his bedsit. He kept expecting the police. What would he tell them? That he'd been there? Seen Danny's throat cut?

He crouched down, pressed the heels of his hands into his eyes. If he could just lose that image. If he could just stop seeing it – seeing his panicky eyes, feeling the warmth of the blood as it spurted from his throat.

It was still there, the blood. He could see it, there on his clothes. On the sleeves of his jumper. He tore everything off – jeans, jumper, underwear. They were all soaked in it, all red, all warm, and the smell . . . He threw them across the room, shuddering, but it was still there, underneath, all over him, over his arms, his hands. He rubbed his palms on the lino, on the bedcovers, on the sofa, ran them down the walls until the whole room was streaked with blood and still his hands were red. It wouldn't come off. Why? Why?

He ran to the bathroom, held his hands under the hot tap, scrubbed at his skin. Blood whirled around the plughole, but his hands were no cleaner. If anything, there was more blood. Where the fuck was it all coming from? Nothing – nothing would get it off. Bleach. Bleach, that would do it. He picked up the bottle from beside the toilet and poured it onto his hand. There was hardly any of it left – not enough. It slimed over his skin. It would take a while to work, wouldn't it? To bleach it off? Wouldn't it? But it didn't go. Still there – the streaks, the splashes, all over him. His legs too, his belly. He looked in the mirror. All over his face. Blood, blood, everywhere.

He fell to the floor and screamed. Stopped almost immediately. That would do nothing, and some nosy neighbour would call the police for sure. He didn't need that. Didn't need them coming in, questioning him – not when the boy's blood was all over him – all over the bedsit, all over everything.

His head spun as he hauled himself to his feet. Bed. He'd go to bed. His feet were red, they splashed in it, waded through warm, thick blood, so thick it sucked at his feet. It would leak through the floor and then everyone would know. Everyone would know he was guilty. Squelch, squelch, his feet went, until they stuck fast. It was up to his knees now, the blood, like a red sea. His hips, his shoulders, then it was lapping around his chin. He lifted his face, breathed, as it poured into his ears. One last breath. One.

'What the fuck are you doing?' Blue eyes stared out of a sickly white face.

Spicer was frozen, so cold, so cold, curled up on the grubby lino floor stained with drips of coffee, splashes of tea. He sat up. 'Where's the blood?'

'What?'

'There was blood. It was . . .' Up to his ears? Drowning him? His hands were red raw but clean, no sign of the streaks. 'I thought . . .'

Art looked away, sighed. 'Get up. Get dressed. We have work to do.'

Spicer scrambled to his feet and pulled on his jeans that were lying where he'd thrown them. 'I'm not doing anything with *you*.' He hopped, one leg in his jeans. 'You bastards. You fucking . . .'

Art groaned. 'Shut up, and get me the priest.'

'*Priest?*' Spicer laughed. He fastened his jeans, sat on the bed and pulled his t-shirt over his head. '*You* want a priest? Are you kidding?'

'If we're going to protect the child from Papa, we'll need him.' Art slipped a hand into the pocket of his jeans, and pulled out a scrap of paper. 'Get him, take him here.' He handed the paper to Spicer. On it was a local postcode. 'If he brings his sidekick, all the better. Get him to bring his books.'

'Books?'

Art blinked, slowly, took a deep breath. 'Try to focus, Spicer, or you'll be no use to me.'

'Right.' Focus. That was what he needed to do. The blood had gone. His hands were clean. All he had to do was keep Art happy, and Papa happy, and everything would be fine.

Art leaned into Spicer's face, stared into his eyes. 'On the back is a floor plan of the building.' He spoke slowly, deliberately, as if talking to an idiot. 'Take him – *them* – to the room with an X on it. I'll meet you there . . .' He glanced at his watch. '. . . in an hour.'

'What if he won't come?'

'Make him. Tell him – tell him the kid's in danger. Tell him anything that'll get him there.'

Spicer drove to the Vicarage. He stared, unblinking, at the road ahead. He parked, climbed out of the car, went through the gates and into the vicarage without thinking about what he'd say, without thinking about anything.

He knocked at the door, sniffed under his arms, wished he'd had time for a shower.

Pearl's mum answered. 'Spicer.' She tried. Her tone was

upbeat, as if seeing him was a pleasant surprise, but the hesitant smile, the worried frown told him it wasn't.

'Hello,' Spicer tried a smile of his own, could imagine how he looked – grey stubble, hair that needed a cut, not to mention a wash. 'Is, um, Luke in?'

'He's in church.' Her frown deepened. 'Is this about Art?'

Spicer's vision wobbled. 'What?'

'He's missing, didn't you know?'

'No,' he said quickly. 'No, it's not about him.'

Silence. He couldn't look at her, didn't know what to say, what to do.

'Did you know he went missing from hospital, Spicer?'

'No.' He forced himself to look in her eyes.

She nodded. 'We're worried.' Her face looked pinched. 'Because – because he's out there somewhere, and we're hoping he won't . . .'

'He won't.' He just wanted to get out of there.

'Pardon?'

'Look, everything's fine. Pearl's fine and Lucas is fine. Everything's . . .'

'Fine?'

He laughed. 'Yeah – just something I wanted to check with Luke, that's all. Nothing to, um . . .' He waved a hand at nothing in particular. 'I'll just mosey on down there.' He laughed again, awkward, nervous.

As he approached the lych gate to the church, a wave of nausea and dizziness came over him. He reached out for the gate, but the wood stung, burned into his hand. 'Fuck's sake!' He pulled his hand away, blew on it. Splinters, that's all it was. Splinters of wood. He breathed, stared at the church door, which stood ajar. Nothing to be afraid of. It was a church. He'd been inside a church before, once or twice. And yet he was afraid – more than afraid. A paralysing dread gripped him at the thought of going in there.

Maybe he could go back, tell Art Luke was out, that he couldn't find him. This was for Lucas though, at least that's what Art had said. So he waited, and waited. He watched the clouds scudding across the darkening blue sky. He watched the jackdaws, or rooks, or whatever they were, gathering on the branches, then flying up, squawking at some invisible trigger. Crows. Big black crows.

He shivered, checked his watch. It was already an hour since he'd left Art. The colour had gone from the sky, and a chill descended as mist formed in amongst the black trees. It wafted like smoke, drifting above the ground. A sudden gust of wind cut through his clothing, lifted the hair from his scalp.

'Shit,' he muttered. 'Shit, shit, shit.' His mouth was dry as once more he reached out a hand. He swallowed, laid his hand on the iron latch of the gate, careful not to touch the wood. Smooth cold metal. He exhaled, breathed, pushed the gate open. The path cut straight through the graveyard. On each side, at regular intervals, were small plaques with names on, dates, inscriptions. In loving memory. In memoriam. Dearly loved, taken from us too soon. Too soon.

He wasn't reading the words any more. He was reciting the inscription on his sister's gravestone. He looked from one side of the path to the other. Never ahead. Never at the building, or at the gaping darkness beyond the open door. Whispers. He could hear them. Coming from inside the church, or outside? He spun around. Nothing. Nothing, but the mist, closing in, silencing the world. There seemed to be only him and that door.

And the voices.

'Spicer.'

He spun around, saw a dark shape coming from the side of the church. His pulse pounded as it came towards him, as it reached for him.

'Maddie said you were looking for me.'

The release from Spicer's lungs made him double over, clutch at his knees. Saliva flooded into his mouth. He was going to throw up. *Not here, not here.*

'Are you all right?' Luke patted his back.

'Yes.' Spicer straightened up, wiped his mouth on his sleeve. 'Yes. Thanks. Sorry.'

Luke's warm eyes watched him. Concern, that's what they showed – no judgement, fear, disgust, just concern. 'Come back to the vicarage and have dinner. You look half-starved.'

'I can't. Thank you, though. I've come to – ask you a favour.'

'Go on.' A guarded tone had crept into his voice.

'Would you come with me? It won't take long.'

'Come with you where?'

'Just, you know . . .' Despite the chill, Spicer's skin prickled with sweat. He shivered. 'Please?'

'Shall I bring Maddie?'

'No.' Too quick, too sharp.

Luke's eyes narrowed. 'What's this about?'

'Can you bring Andrew?'

Luke took a step back, inhaled and let it out, slowly.

'Okay,' he said. 'Will I need my bible, my . . ?'

'I don't know. Yes.' Spicer glanced at the gate, except it wasn't there any more, shrouded in fog. 'Yes, bring everything.'

Luke nodded, pulled his phone from his pocket, tapped the screen and held it to his ear. 'Andrew? I'm sorry to disturb you on your day off but I think we may have a problem.'

26. SPICER

Five minutes later, they were driving, Andrew in the front passenger seat, Luke in the back.

The streets grew shabbier as they drove. Boarded-up shops nestled alongside lap dancing clubs and take-aways. Further on, they came to a terrace of four-storey town houses that must once have been respectable. Now they were flats or bed and breakfast hostels. Their white-painted fronts streaked with dirt. Rubbish bags strewn seemingly at random. Spicer turned into a narrow alleyway between two terraces, and then right into a back lane. Once, the fences had no doubt been well cared-for, but most were now broken down, or non-existent. The only evidence they'd ever been there, the wooden posts, some at an angle, some laying flat. Spicer stopped for a moment, checked the scrap of paper, looked up. It was the right place.

Luke was already out of the car. 'Which house?'

Spicer pointed.

Luke ran, stumbling across the uneven ground towards the back of a particularly dilapidated house. Two men stood outside, voices raised, gesticulating wildly. Their clothes, even their skin had the look of ingrained dirt, of living on the streets.

'Luke.' Spicer legged it after him, Andrew close behind.

Luke turned his head, paused. 'Tell me Pearl's not here.'

'I . . .' Various options ran through Spicer's head. If Luke knew she wasn't there, would he back out? 'I can't,' he said at last. Not a lie as such.

Luke made a strange noise, a mixture of horror and

despair.

A pang of guilt stung Spicer. Luke had been so good to him, and now – now, he would maybe pay for that with his life.

Rubbish littered the bare hallway. A hollow-eyed girl lay asleep or unconscious, her back against the wall, covered with a filthy sleeping bag. Music throbbed through the ceiling. Now and again laughter, or curses. The smell was almost overpowering, of human waste overlaid with stale alcohol, and burning paper.

'Here.' Spicer opened a heavy metal door. It seemed out of place in the ramshackle house. The one item of any substance.

The room was bare, but for a single chair fixed to the concrete floor. The walls looked like some kind of modern art, with patches of bare plaster, interspersed with sections of layered wallpaper. Years and years captured like an archaeological dig, unveiling patterns long obsolete, out of fashion, dated. Spicer was taken aback. Where was Art? Was it a trap? A trick?

Next to the chair, coiled on the floor, each fixed at one end to a ring embedded in the floor, were chains – four of them. A small pile of padlocks lay next to them.

Andrew backed away, into the corridor. Art appeared behind him, pushed him into the room, and locked the door behind them.

'Spicer?' Luke's confusion changed to crushing disappointment.

'Sorry.' Spicer couldn't look at him, couldn't look at any of them, least of all Art, who held his hand out to the priests. 'Your phones?'

Luke pulled his from a pocket and handed it over.

'Sorry,' Spicer said again to no one in particular. To everyone.

'What were you thinking?' Andrew slapped his phone into Art's waiting hand.

'Sorry.' What else could he say? How had he let Art talk him into this?

'The Lord be with us,' Luke said. 'The Lord make his face to shine upon us. Yea, though we walk through . . .'

'Yes, yes.' Art held up a hand. 'Enough.' He sat on the only chair.

Luke and Andrew turned to Spicer but he could only shrug. He knew no more than they did.

'Spicer,' Art's eyes burned, feverish. The blue dulled as red veins spread across the whites of his eyes.

Something ran over Spicer's skin, crawling, like hundreds of tiny insects. The room felt suddenly airless.

'Here.' Art handed him the key to the door and the two phones. 'Do not give these up, to them or to me, no matter *what* I tell you.'

'What?'

'If I order you to unchain me, don't do it.' Art winced.

'Unchain *you?*'

Art's jaw clenched. 'Get on with it.' An unhealthy sheen covered his sallow skin. 'Make it secure.'

Spicer picked up the chains. They weighed heavy in his hands. 'I can't . . .'

Andrew snatched them from him.

Art's eyes, bloodshot and weeping, slid to Luke. 'You *can* do this, yes?'

'Is Pearl safe?'

'Yes.'

'And Lucas?'

Art nodded. 'But not for long, if you don't do this.'

Luke shook his head. 'You could have just asked, instead of . . .' He waved an arm to encompass the room.

'Would you have come?' Art said.

'Of course.'

'For me?' Art snorted. 'No chance.'

Andrew cuffed Art's hands to the chair. He wound the heavy chains around him.

'Tighter,' Art said. 'Make it so I can't move.'

Spicer wiped the sweat from his brow. He wasn't sure if the room was warm, or if it was him. There was something claustrophobic about the windowless walls, although it wasn't a small room, and the ceiling was high. Plenty of air. Plenty of oxygen.

'Or bite,' Art said.

Spicer bent and picked up the leather strap from the floor. He stared at it.

'Do it.' Art's skin was grey, his lips colourless.

'You're not well,' Spicer said. He turned to Luke. 'He's ill.'

'No.' Luke took the gag from Spicer's hand, tied it across Art's mouth. 'This is normal. This is just the beginning.' He glanced up at Spicer, and frowned. 'You look pale yourself. Are you all right?'

Nausea washed over Spicer. 'Feel a bit . . .' The walls seemed to vibrate. 'It's too hot.'

Art made a sound. His eyes widened.

Andrew touched Spicer's arm. His hand burned through his jacket, stung his skin. 'Shit.' He snatched his arm away.

'Sit down,' Luke said. 'There's a long way to go yet. Did you bring in the aspergillum?'

'Asper what?'

'The water and sprinkler.'

Spicer shook his head. 'No – I mean. I don't know. Was it in the car?'

'Yes,' Luke said. 'A bottle and a stick with a silver ball on the end, remember?'

'Yeah. Yeah, of course.' Had there been water? He'd seen a blue-topped plastic bottle somewhere, maybe sitting on the back seat. But it could have been a dream, could have been an ad on TV for all he knew.

'I'll, er . . .' He headed for the door. It swayed in front of him. Dehydration, that's what it was. That would explain it. He found the keyhole with some difficulty, turned the key, and almost fell out into the corridor. Art was making sounds behind him – urgent, panicky.

He locked the door behind him. Had to be careful – very careful. He felt his way, one hand on the wall. The buzzing was growing again. They were awake, stretching, their antennae twitching. 'No, no,' he said. 'I'm on it. I'm . . .'

The car was still intact, wheels and all. Maybe people knew. They'd be afraid of Mesmeris, afraid of *him* if they had any sense. He laughed aloud, thought how weird it sounded, echoing back from somewhere – the walls, outer space. He laughed again, and again, louder each time, until the buzzing in his head reached a crescendo, drowning out his voice. He was meant to be doing something, for Art, or Papa. Something . . . The car. Blue-capped bottle. That was it. Water. He reached into the car and pulled the bottle and asper-whatever out. Clasping them against his chest, he rested his back against the car and looked up at the night sky – clear now, with stars but no moon.

A big universe out there. Endless places to hide. He could run away, go anywhere, anywhere he wanted. There was no warrant out for his arrest. He had no criminal record, nothing to stop him starting again, making a new life, forgetting the past.

He climbed into the car and put the key in the ignition. Pain made him cry out – excruciating, stabbing pains down his arms, like someone sticking needles into his nerves. Deep, like being skewered over and over again. His legs, his neck, back, head, the piercing went on and on, and on. The pain made him faint, nauseous.

'All right.' He pulled the key out, opened the driver's door and fell onto the gravel, shoulder first. The bottle and sprinkler rolled across the ground. 'All *right.*' Slowly, slowly, he got to his feet and bent to pick them up, one hand on the car for balance.

A few seconds of deep breathing and the pain eased. Even the buzzing quietened. Now he'd got it right. Pleasing Papa, pleasing Papa, that was the thing. As he headed back to the house, his mind cleared. Other noises registered, noises from outside his head. People talking, music, planes flying overhead, traffic. Too much noise. Everywhere, everywhere noise.

'Shut up,' he shouted. 'Shut the fuck up.'

They weren't that afraid of him then. Well, they would be, once they got to know him, these people making all that row.

The two priests were pacing the floor, Luke reading

something aloud from a book in his hand. Impossible to hear what it was, with Art yelling incoherently, struggling against the chains, against the gag.

He stopped when he saw Spicer, and slumped back in the chair. *You thought I wasn't coming back, didn't you? And you were almost right.* Spicer locked the door, and slipped the key into his pocket. He handed the things to Andrew, flinched as the priest's hand brushed his.

'Why don't you sit down?' Andrew said. 'You look dead beat.'

A powerful urge came over him to put his hands around Andrew's neck and squeeze the life out of him. An urge so strong he had to clasp his hands together, had to look away, had to push it down. 'Yeah,' he said, and his voice sounded weird to him, other, deeper and rougher than usual. Dehydration, must be. It could cause hallucinations, couldn't it? Or was that hypothermia? Something anyway. He wiped his mouth with the back of his hand and wished he had a bottle of water, wished he'd drunk the one the priests had. He looked up, straight into Art's bloodshot eyes.

He knew. Art knew. Knew exactly what was going on in Spicer's head, and he could do nothing about it. It frightened Spicer, the way he felt, the wild elation building inside him. He felt strong, potent, dangerous.

He sat in the corner, leaned his head back against the wall and closed his eyes. If he could just block out the noise, think himself on a beach somewhere, or on a mountain, surrounded by trickling streams, birdsong, buzzing insects. If he could make himself imagine the smell of heather and gorse, of crushed grass. If he could do that, then . . .

Screams woke him – piercing, loud – followed by whimpers. He'd been in bed, he was sure of it, so why was he sitting on a hard concrete floor. Then it all came back. The screams belonged to who? Art? Andrew? Spicer's eyes were fogged. He squinted, rubbed at them, squinted again. Darkness – shapes moved in a shadow dance. Silhouettes loomed up to the ceiling, lunged at him. Spicer cowered, shuffled back, made himself small, while the cries went on. He closed his eyes. This dream was no good. No good.

A hush descended, and in the hush, came whispers – in his head or real, he couldn't tell. Someone was telling him something. A warning about Andrew, about the words. He held his breath, but still couldn't make out what they were saying. He got the gist though. Someone was trying to harm Papa. That was the gist, the problem. Those bastard priests were trying to destroy everything.

Through the whispering came other sounds – a low, male voice chanting something – foul words that made Spicer's skin prickle, made his guts churn, and then Art, not screaming this time, not moaning, but talking. Talking – about Papa, about . . .

Spicer opened his eyes a fraction, peered into the darkness. There was Art, still strapped to the chair, but the gag was gone, and his mouth was moving, telling them everything, about Papa, about the people he'd killed, tortured. Now and again, Andrew or Luke made small sounds, groans. Devil sounds, enemy sounds. But Andrew wasn't the real danger. No, the real danger was Luke, Luke and Art. Spicer realised what he had to do. He had to stop them. That's what the whispers were saying. He . . .

He stumbled to his feet. The room swayed, tilted. He fell against the wall. Why wouldn't they stay still, the bastards? He steadied himself, took one step towards them.

Luke's back was to him, and he was mumbling stuff – mumbo jumbo, religious crap. Spicer laughed as he lunged forwards.

His face smacked onto the concrete floor with a crack. Pain radiated around his head, pain and noise – was it him, or them? Get up. He had to get up, had to stop them, but something pinned him to the floor. He turned his head. Wet, the floor was wet. It soaked his skin. He couldn't see. A dog collar. The enemy was on his back. Andrew pulled his arms back and wrapped a chain around them. His hands pressed on the back of Spicer's head, pushed his face into the floor, into the blood, and snot, and dust. He couldn't breathe.

He had to get up, had to stop Art blabbing, had to shut him the fuck up, to save Papa. But his feet were shackled too, the chained wrapped around a massive radiator pipe. He roared, tried to drown out Art's treacherous words, his confession.

Something flew through the air towards him, something dark. He screamed. Opening his mouth was a mistake. The enemy whipped a gag over it, tied it behind his head.

And all he could do was listen, listen as Art confessed everything. Now and again, Andrew groaned, and Spicer wondered if he was going to throw up all over him. Vomit to mix with the blood.

Art's words turned to sobs, and Spicer knew it was too late. Then the chants started, the vile words that bored into his brain and made his insides squirm. 'I exorcise you, every unclean spirit.' They went on and on. Andrew chanted them too, his burning hands on Spicer's scalp. 'And to you, oh devil, begone.'

Spicer felt something being drawn from him. A jolt of fear hit him, that it was his life, his life-force leaving his body. He had to hold on to it, stop it happening. He clung to it and cried out. He heard Art cry out at the same moment, and this thing, this whatever it was, was ripped out through his mouth. It tore at his being, flayed his insides.

His face was so wet. Tears and blood, saliva and snot pooled around him.

The thing, the thing inside of him, passed his chest. He choked, coughed at the pain. He sobbed, great, hacking sobs, for everything he'd lost.

Water everywhere. It trickled over his head, and into his mouth. He was going to drown. Maybe this was their plan, the priests, to drown him.

He knew he was meant to be doing something, something important – something for Papa. He had to do it before he died, he knew that, but he couldn't remember what it was, or why. Why would he help Papa, when Papa was evil?

He cried for his sister, for his mother, for all the victims of Papa's hatred.

The weight disappeared from his back.

'Sorry about that.' Andrew removed the gag and took the cuffs from his ankles, the chain from his hands. 'You could have told us you'd been inducted.'

'I couldn't.' Spicer rubbed at his wrists, at the itching, bloodied skin. He shifted to a sitting position and leaned his head back against the wall. He felt completely empty, and weak. 'What *was* that?'

'We don't know,' Luke said. 'We only know it's gone.'

Spicer's laugh ended in a choked sob. 'You mean we're free?'

'For now.'

Art sat slumped in the chair, head bowed, chin on his chest. He stirred, groaned.

Andrew put an arm around his shoulders, perhaps afraid he'd topple from the chair.

'You're okay,' he said.

Art nodded, just once, opened his eyes and straightened up. He looked the same as ever – hard-faced, dead eyes. He stood. Spicer detected a slight wobble, but when Luke put a hand out to steady him, Art brushed it off. 'I'm fine,' he said, irritated. 'Spicer.' He beckoned him with one finger. 'We need to get back.' He held out a hand. 'Key.'

'What?'

'Hold on a minute,' Luke said. 'Where are you going?'

'We're taking you back,' Art said, his voice slow, patient. 'Then we're going to get cleaned up.'

'Right.' Luke frowned. 'You'll need to rest.'

'Yeah, yeah.' Art took the keys, unlocked the door and led them back to the car.

The two priests climbed in the back. Art sat in the front passenger seat, Spicer in the driver's. He tried to grip the steering wheel, but his hands shook so much, one tremor after another, that he couldn't hold it. *Breathe. Breathe and calm down. One, two, three.*

'We need to get moving,' Art said.

'I'm trying.' Spicer clenched his jaw, concentrated on

keeping his hands still. He laid them on the steering wheel, tried to bend his fingers. They wouldn't grip. Why wouldn't they grip? It was as if he'd lost control of his own body. 'Shit!' He looked over his shoulder. 'What's happened to me?'

'It's just shock,' Andrew said. 'It won't last.'

'Great.' Spicer wanted to cry.

He swapped seats with Art. It seemed the shock hadn't affected *him* at all. No trembling hands, no problem gripping the wheel. The relief and elation Spicer had felt immediately after the exorcism faded to utter exhaustion.

They pulled up outside the vicarage, and the two priests climbed out.

Luke bent to Art's window. 'If you want to survive, I suggest you leave the country – preferably tonight.'

Art smiled. 'I have one or two things to sort out first.'

Luke's eyes narrowed. 'Don't go near them, either of you. You can be re-infected.'

'We know,' Art said.

Spicer shivered. Never again did he want to hear that buzzing in his head, feel his insides torn apart.

'God bless you,' Luke said, making the sign of the cross.

'God bless you, my arse,' Art muttered as they drove away through the country lanes.

Spicer stared out at the fields and woodland. 'Where are we going?'

'Back in. Where d'you think we're going?'

'You're kidding.'

Art ignored him.

'You heard what Luke said. We'll get re-infected.' He considered grabbing the steering wheel, crashing the car into a brick wall. Even that was a better prospect that going back to Papa's, but there was no brick wall – only hedges and trees and ditches.

Art shot him a sideways glance. 'You said you wanted to keep the child safe from Papa.'

'You know I do.'

Art shrugged. 'Then we protect him from inside, unless you have a better idea?'

A rhetorical question. There was no other way. Spicer knew that, but it didn't stop his bowels turning to water at the thought of it. 'Will he know – Papa? Know we've been exorcised?'

'If he does, we're dead.'

'Brilliant.' The nightmare never ended. Never.

The house looked ghostly in the moonlight, almost unreal, an ethereal vision rather than solid stone. Papa's black limo stood parked outside.

They parked the car and climbed out. Spicer wanted to run, wanted to get as far away as he could from that place and never come back. The only thing that stopped him was one small boy. He couldn't let Lucas down, not if he wanted to live with himself. Decision made, he climbed the steps and pushed the front door open.

Leo stood at the top of the stairs like a grotesque parody of himself. His knuckles stood out white as he gripped the stair rail.

'If you're staying,' he said, 'close the door. It's fucking freezing.'

Spicer shut the world out, shut himself in, with them.

'That'll teach you to try and nick my kid,' Art said, with a smirk.

'It's not *your* kid,' Leo snarled. 'It's Papa's.'

A nerve twitched in Art's jaw.

Figures emerged from Papa's study – Ruby, Malki and finally Papa himself.

Art dropped to his knees. Spicer wondered if he should do the same but it was too late. He'd left it too long. Not that Papa seemed to mind. He walked straight past Art, the white cross around his neck swinging from side to side like a pendulum. He slapped his arm around Spicer's shoulder. 'Here he is, our secret weapon.'

Spicer's skin crawled.

'You've found our traitor.' Papa's lip curled in a sneer as he looked down at Art's bowed head. 'Excellent work, Spicer. Excellent.'

Spicer's mouth dried up, his heart fluttered. Would Art think he'd betrayed him – to Papa?

Leo clomped down the stairs. 'What're we going to do with him?'

'The cellar,' Papa said.

Ruby and Malki dragged Art away. Leo followed, the gun in his hand trained on Art's head. So much for going back in and ruining Papa's plans from the inside. Cheers, Art, Spicer thought. Cheers for dropping me right in the shit.

They gave Spicer a pokey room at the back of the house. It smelled of the emulsion that had been haphazardly slapped onto the walls, obviously in a hurry since patches of it were still tacky.

He unpacked his clothes and sat on the bed. Moisture chilled the air. Even the mattress felt damp. A sink stood in the corner of the room and beside it, a plastic cabinet. On top of that lay soap, shampoo, a toothbrush and mouthwash. Was this going to be his life now? They were going to kill Art. That much had been obvious. What he needed to do now was to keep himself alive, because dead he'd be no use to anyone.

He swilled his mouth with the pink mouthwash, combed his hair and went downstairs. The hallway was empty, but voices came from a door at the far end. It stood ajar, warm, orange light spilling into the darkened hallway. He pushed the door open, a hard lump at the back of his throat.

He was back with them and he was on his own.

27. PEARL

I was convinced Art would come back, that he hadn't run away but had a plan, a scheme to put everything right. My fantasy Art would be doing that. He'd have a good heart under that shell. I waited all night. In the morning, I washed and changed my clothes, stared at myself in the mirror. A hollow-eyed ghoul stared back. I tried calling Spicer. No reply. I left a message, remembered to ask how he was first, before asking if he knew where Art was. It would annoy him but that was tough. There was no one else.

Lucas must have picked up on my nervousness because he was more awkward than he'd ever been. When I asked what he wanted for breakfast, he folded his arms across his chest.

'Nothing.'

'Lucas. You need to eat.'

'I'm ill.' He lowered his chin and frowned.

'What's the matter?'

'I told you,' he said. 'The worms.'

'Shut up.' *Would he never stop going on about them?* 'Just shut up about the bloody worms.'

Mum and Dad came over and tried to convince me to move back home for a while.

'At least until they find Art,' Mum said.

A little electric shock went through me at the mention of his name.

'He's no threat to me, Mum. He's had years to get in touch and he never has, so why would he bother now?'

Sane question, I thought. Sensible even, and best of all, they didn't have an answer for it.

'Have you seen the doctor?' Mum's forehead wrinkled in worry.

'Yes. Yes,' I lied. 'And I'm fine. Just a blip, she said.'

'That's good.' Mum nodded but the frown didn't budge. 'You don't look well though.'

'I'm *fine.*' It was so hard to stop my jaw clenching. I was desperate to get them out of there in case Art came back, but at the same time, I was trying to appear relaxed. It was hopeless – hopeless. I kept visualising them bumping into each other on the path to the house, in the living room, outside on the street, and imagining what would happen then, and it made me shake, the thought of it.

Mum glanced at Dad. 'Er, shall *I* make the tea?' she said.

'Sorry.' Of course they'd want tea. They always did. 'Sorry. I'll make it.' At least I could watch the road out of the window then – keep a look out.

Dad followed me into the kitchen. Damn it.

I filled the kettle, glanced outside. Nothing. The road was quiet.

Dad cleared his throat. He had his hands clasped together and that look on his face, the wary one, so I knew what was coming. 'We still need to . . .'

I jumped in before he could get going. 'He hasn't mentioned them again,' I lied, 'so I really don't think . . .'

Lucas appeared in the doorway. 'Grandma's going to take me to nursery.'

'Oh, right.' I'd planned to keep him home, but couldn't think of a decent reason for doing so. Anyway, he wanted to go, and maybe if I had a quiet house I'd be able to think.

Maybe. So I let them, and then worried that they'd exorcise him behind my back, which was ridiculous. They'd never do that, not Mum and Dad. Still, I couldn't settle. If that scratch was a mini Mesmeris mark, then nursery wasn't safe. Several times I decided to pick him up, to make some excuse about a doctor's appointment or the dentist. Each time, just as I reached my car, I'd imagine Art coming back, finding the house empty, and I'd go back inside. Finally, I picked Lucas up at the usual time. He seemed absolutely normal. There was nothing wrong with him at all. Nothing.

Only once we got back home did he start playing up. Was it a sign, his tetchiness? A symptom of Papa's influence? Or was he just tired? Everything Lucas did suddenly seemed portentous – a frown, a puzzled look, an unusual word. He'd be learning new words at nursery, of course. Of course he would. I was looking too hard, searching for Papa in my own child. I'd take him to Dad, I thought. Otherwise we'd grow apart, me and Lucas, separated by doubt and suspicion. I'd take him even though it made me feel ill to think of it, my baby going through an exorcism.

Perhaps it would be best to wait a few days, I thought. Give Art time to arrange whatever he was arranging, just in case Lucas didn't need to go through it. Just in case there was another way.

Yes, that would be the best thing. That would be sensible.

*

The days went by – two or three of them. I lived on autopilot, concentrated on the small things, what to have for dinner, what to wear, what TV programmes to watch. The days went by like that, all dullness except for Lucas, but even he felt tainted by Mesmeris and I couldn't relax properly around him no matter how I tried. I didn't want him to think I'd stopped loving him, but that's how it must have seemed. I hadn't of course. I was just afraid. By Friday afternoon, with the weekend looming ahead – two whole days with no nursery, I knew I had to take him to Dad. There was no other way.

I'd already made the decision when I saw the note – a white envelope laying on the doormat. The post never came that late in the afternoon. I watched it for a moment, as if expecting it to jump up and attack me. I edged towards it, flipped it over with my shoe.

My stomach tightened. That writing, sharp, angular, aggressive, made me afraid although I didn't know why. No stamp. Hand-delivered.

I left it there while I made a cup of tea, hoping it would disappear. I made Lucas a pizza, his favourite. Every time I walked from the miniscule kitchen to the living room, my eye went straight to the letter.

While Lucas ate, the tightness in my belly grew worse. I stood, paced to the doorway. It was still there, white and poisonous, the black, jagged handwriting somehow obscene on that pure white paper. I cleared Lucas's plate away, washed it up, took him a glass of milk.

The longer I left it, the worse I felt. I stepped forward, bent and picked it up. I felt as if my heart might stop, or burst right out of my chest, or my mouth. The beats thumped so hard, it hurt. *Breathe – just breathe. What's the worst it can be? Words – it's words, that's all. Probably a party invitation for Lucas.* I slipped my finger under the loose edge, biting hard on my lip to stop it twitching. I tore the envelope open. One sheet of cheap, lined paper, folded in two.

'Mummy?'

I made a garbled sound, unfolded the paper, breathing through my mouth, light-headed.

My brain struggled to decipher the words, never mind meaning in the erratic, barbed scrawl. No attempt had been made to fit the words into the narrow lines. Instead they strayed at random across the page.

They're coming for the child. Go to your parents.

The signature, a solitary, sharp, stiletto-like A, pierced the paper. Its end pointed like a weapon, an arrow.

It couldn't be him. I knew that. He wouldn't leave a letter. He'd have knocked, come in, spoken to me face to face.

'Mummy, there's the man.'

'Mmm?' *The child,* it said. Art's words. *The child,* as if he'd been bought from a supermarket, as if the child wasn't his son, but an object, a thing.

'Mummy!' Lucas yelled, pointing a finger at the television.

'What?' I shouted back. 'What the . . ?'

There, on the screen, sat Papa with his cruel, weak mouth. His black eyes stared right at me. It was a clip from the interview I'd already seen.

Lucas said something.

'Shush.'

Papa laughed. It felt as if he was in the room, laughing at us, at me. I didn't remember him laughing like that, not laughing at me like that.

I pressed the off switch, and the screen went blank.

My voice sounded shrill. 'What a funny man.'

'He was at nursery,' Lucas said, a cross frown drawing his eyebrows together. 'That's why I wanted you to see, and you wouldn't listen.'

'What?' I held his shoulders.

'You were staring at your paper . . .'

I shook him. 'What did you say?'

His lip wobbled. His blue, blue eyes swam with tears.

'Sorry.' I picked him up from his chair and hugged him. 'I'm sorry, but – *that* man . . .' I pointed a shaking finger at the television. 'That man was – was . . ? Oh, my God!'

'What's the matter?'

'Nothing.' I looked at the letter again. I tried Spicer's number. No reply.

I ran to the bedroom. 'Come on, Lucas.'

He turned his head, but didn't move.

'We're going away for a while.' I grabbed his elbow, lifted him to his feet. 'That's nice, isn't it? A holiday?'

He may have been three years old, but he wasn't stupid. His mouth turned right down. 'Don't want to.'

'Tough.'

I ran around the flat, throwing things – clothes, toiletries, toys into bags. The whole time, Lucas whined.

'What are you doing? Where are we going? Why are you taking my toys?' On and on, and on.

I couldn't answer him, because my throat was choked with fear. Any minute, they could break in – any minute.

Lucas cried then, properly, silently, big, ploppy tears running down his face.

I scooped him up in my arms and kissed his teary cheek. 'It's all right, baby. It's all going to be all right I promise, okay?' I tilted his chin, forced him to look at me. 'Okay?' I did my best reassuring smile.

Once the bags were packed in the boot, I turned all the switches off, turned off the heating. I tried Spicer again. Straight to answerphone. I left a voicemail, told him where we'd be.

I strapped Lucas into his car seat, climbed into the driver's seat, and shut my door. It was dark already.

At the end of the road, I checked behind me. Nothing. No smooth, black saloon or red Fiesta. My tummy muscles ached, so I consciously relaxed them, made myself breathe. I pulled out onto the main road. A car came right up behind me, too close, blinding full beam headlights, tailgating. Shit! I changed the angle of my rear-view mirror, and swerved left into a side street. They didn't follow, but roared past, bass rhythm pulsating around them. I pulled into the kerb and breathed deeply until my pulse settled and my hands stopped shaking enough to carry on. 'Idiot,' I said. 'What a prat of a driver.'

Back on the main street and I had it to myself. No traffic this time, an empty road. I drove through the country lanes, calmed by the emptiness, the solitude. We drove through patchy fog. I raised myself up a little and glanced in the rear-view mirror. Lucas was fast asleep already. As I turned my attention back to the road ahead, something caught my eye – a glimmer of light behind us.

The car bumped over uneven ground as I clipped the

verge. I righted it, glanced in the mirror again. Nothing – no headlights.

The moon broke through the fog for a moment, and I checked again.

A car – a car full of people. No lights. Idiots, or . . .

Lads, I told myself – maybe drunk, showing off.

We jolted forwards.

They'd hit the back of my car. Not lads, then. Not lads.

I put my foot to the floor, gripped the steering wheel, focussed on the road in front. Not far – not far to go. The lights of the village twinkled up ahead, through the trees. Minutes, that's all – just minutes and we'd be there.

The speed dial went up – sixty, seventy, eighty. The old car vibrated at the unfamiliar speed. *Please don't fail me now – not now.*

It seemed I'd lost them. Quick glances in the mirror showed no glimmers. Moonlight reflected off the empty road behind me.

'Thank you, God.' I eased my foot off the accelerator, just a little, so the car stopped juddering.

'Almost there,' I said, aloud. 'We're almost there.'

Mist descended from nowhere. I slowed a little more. Movement to my right made my skin prickle.

I saw them just as their car slammed into the side of mine. It ricocheted back, then came at me again.

Nowhere to go. Nowhere.

'Mummy,' Lucas yelled.

Another huge thump and we were on the verge, bumping over the rough ground.

The steering wheel twisted. I couldn't hold it, couldn't stop it.

'Mummy!'

I braked, as the car went over the bank. God! God! It was as if someone had hold of the steering wheel, was wresting it from my grasp.

We headed straight for the trees.

This is it, I thought. The end.

I swerved to avoid a huge tree trunk and the car tilted, tipped forwards, hurtled down a bank and died.

'Lucas?' I undid my seat belt, leaned over the back. 'Lucas.'

He whimpered.

'It's all right, baby.'

I freed him from the car seat, took him into my arms.

'Shush now, Lucas. *Shush*!' I heaved him over the seats, opened the door and rolled out, crouched over my boy. 'If you make a noise, they'll find us, d'you understand?'

He nodded, eyes huge in the darkness.

'I need you to be very, very quiet, and very, very good, okay?'

Another nod.

A shout rang out. 'There.'

I ran. My chest screamed for air, and I was breathing, as fast and hard as I was able. My feet flew over the earth, each footfall jarring my bones, my joints, punching my head. Through my mouth, the moisture-laden air clogged my airways, drowning me slowly. Lucas was heavy in my arms. My chin bumped the top of his head as I ran.

The pain was too much. I stopped, looked for somewhere to hide. Too much choice. Too many trees, but I had to choose, and my breathing – heaving, rasping, was too loud in the still night. It filled my head, so I couldn't hear if they were right behind me or further off.

I stumbled down a bank. It was steeper than it looked, and I slipped, slid on my back over rocks and mud and grass, clinging onto my precious cargo. And there was our hiding place, where the river had eaten away at the bank and made a cavern underneath a huge oak, its tangled roots creating a haven – or a cage, a trap.

There was no choice now. The vibrations from their pounding feet reached me through the earth as they searched, calling to each other, cursing, laughing.

We huddled inside the earth. Like a womb it cradled us, but the chill damp seeped through my clothes, through my flesh, into my bones, and I knew it was the same for Lucas. His small body shuddered every few seconds, and yet he made no sound, not a peep. My little man, my brave boy.

They were right there, above us, so close I could hear their panting.

The river was no more than a stream. It hadn't rained for weeks, and now this sea mist, or fog - ear-numbing, silencing, oxygen-sucking fog. The air unmoving, static, as if the world had stopped and we were left, breathing in our own muck.

'Split up,' a voice said.

I kept still, felt Lucas's heart beat against my chest. I kissed his head. It felt cold against my lips.

Footsteps moved away, voices faded, but someone was still there. I could hear him breathing.

Lucas kept quiet. He was as scared as I was. Every second or two a judder ran through his small body. I felt it, the vibration. I would have undressed him, put him inside my own clothes, but I was afraid to move. The evening was so still, every sound was magnified.

'I know you're here,' a voice whispered. Was it Art? It sounded like him. 'You can come out now. They've gone.' Art, Spicer, I'd trusted them both too many times – never again. I held a finger to my lips and shook my head. Lucas's big eyes stared up at me.

'Pearl, come on,' the voice was more muffled, distant. 'They're bringing dogs.'

Lucas gasped. I clamped my hand to his mouth, held my breath.

'It's okay,' I whispered in Lucas's ear. 'No dogs. He's lying.' And I hoped, prayed it was true.

My boy was so cold. His skin was icy against mine. His shivering was constant. He started to cry – silent, juddery tears.

'Okay,' I whispered. 'Okay. He's gone.' He must have gone, surely. I'd heard nothing for minutes that seemed like hours. My muscles had seized up, so as I straightened my back, pain radiated up my spine. The fog had thinned a little, and spots of rain hit my face as we left our shelter.

I put Lucas on his feet, but his legs folded, so I lifted him again, and clambered up the bank, clinging to branches and tussocks of grass, until we reached the top. 'You have to walk, Lucas,' I said.

He slid his hand into mine. His little legs struggled to keep up. I hurried, but I'd lost all sense of direction. Lucas tripped. I bent to catch him.

A shadow swooped from the darkness and scooped him up, and they were gone, running away from me, into the trees.

I think I screamed – or was it Lucas? Then I stopped

screaming, because I needed all my energy to run. I kept him in sight, the bastard, the child thief. His legs were long, much longer than mine, and they covered more ground. I was powered by love and fear, and I kept him in sight, just.

The trees thinned and ahead was tarmac, a road. Across the road a silver car waited, its engine running, its exhaust adding to the fog.

Two silhouettes appeared by the car. For one crazy moment, I thought a miracle had happened, that God had sent police or angels or whatever to save us. I yelled, 'Stop him!'

Laughter came back to me through the trees. The man with Lucas turned. I thought he was smiling, although it was too dark to see. Still, I thought he smiled, victorious, gloating. He got into the back seat of the car with my baby.

'Stop.' The two figures watched as I ran, my breath coming in ragged gasps.

I was almost there – almost there.

One of them held something in their hand. They pointed it at me. Spray hit my face.

'Lucas.' I screamed it. 'Lucas.'

My foot hit the tarmac. The doors slammed shut. The engine revved. 'No.' A few strides and . . . I reached out. My fingertips brushed metal as the car moved away.

*

The red lights grew smaller and smaller until they were swallowed up by the fog.

I stood there in the middle of the deserted road. The fog turned to fine drizzle and still I stood, still I stared. My brain was numb like the rest of me. Perhaps, if I stood still enough, I thought, if I didn't breathe, then perhaps God would take pity on me and bring my boy back. He wasn't going to do that though, was he? No one was going to do that. *I* had to do it. *I* had to get him back. It felt as if my Doc Martens were made of lead. My right foot slapped onto the tarmac. Then the left, then the right again. One foot in front of the other, that was all I had to do, keep putting one foot in front of the other. To stay there and die would be to let them win – all of them – all the bastards who'd tried to kill me. I wasn't going to do that. I wouldn't give them the satisfaction.

What was it with me, always losing the people I loved? It wasn't true what they said, better to have loved and lost than never to have loved at all. No, no, it wasn't true. Better to have never loved. Too late now. Too late.

The road was longer than I remembered it. On and on I walked. Not a single car drove down it. The friendly lights of the village had gone. It was as if I'd landed on another, uninhabited planet.

I'd go to my parents, I thought. They'd call the police. Everything would be fine. I sped up, keeping to the verge, turned left at a fork in the road. A brook ran down each side of it. I'd never noticed that before, shooting past in my warm bubble of a car. The sound of the water babbling by reminded me of something, something else I'd lost, a long time ago. I wouldn't go there. No. No, not there.

On I went until the soft glow of streetlights pierced the mist. I ran the last bit, tripping over myself. I fell against their door, hammered at it with my fists.

The light inside dazzled my eyes. Music blared from the TV, and it was hot, so hot.

Dad said something, but the cold had numbed my ears. His angry face loomed in front of me. 'Where is he?' he screamed.

Lydia and Mum watched from the doorway to the living room. The way their eyes popped, everything about their faces said they were scared. Scared of me?

'What?' I tried to move towards them, but Dad held me back.

'Lucas,' Dad said. 'Where is he?'

I shook my head.

'Oh, my God!' Mum covered her face with her hands. 'Oh!' She turned her back, bent double. Lydia put an arm around her shoulders and said something.

'They took him,' I said.

Why did they stare like that? As if they hated me?

Dad grabbed my hands. 'What have you done?'

'What?' I had blood on my hands. '*What?*' I stared at the spatters, the streaks. 'I didn't. I haven't . . .'

Spicer burst through the door behind me, all windswept, red-faced.

'There you are,' he said, all out of breath. 'Why did you leave?'

'What?'

'Where's Lucas?' Mum said. 'What's she done?'

'Lucas is fine, don't worry.' Spicer put an arm around my shoulder, squeezed me. 'You're covered in paint – look at you.'

Paint? Why would they spray me with paint? 'They've

taken him,' I said.

Spicer lowered his voice, talked across me to Mum and Dad. 'Lucas is with a friend of mine from the nick. She has two kids the same age.' He had that voice on – the one he used when he thought I was losing it – the patient one. 'They were having a brilliant time playing with a paint gun and then . . .' He squeezed me again, took a deep breath. 'Papa came on the TV. I think it spooked her.'

Spooked who? Me? Had it? *Had* I gone crazy? I didn't feel crazy. Panicked, yes, confused, frightened but not crazy.

Spicer was a good liar, but I knew him. The edges of his lips were white. His arm around me was strong, reassuring, but the way his heart was clattering about wasn't. The way his body trembled wasn't. He was lying, but he seemed to know what he was doing, so I went along with it. I didn't seem to have any choice.

'I'm sorry,' I said. 'I must have . . .'

Mum headed for the phone. 'We'll get the doctor.'

'No.' Spicer and I both said it at once.

'I'll look after her,' Spicer said. 'I'll look after *them.*'

Surprisingly, Mum backed down. Perhaps she couldn't face the trauma of coping with another of my wobblies. Dad frowned at Spicer. 'You haven't been . . ?'

'No,' Spicer said.

'Been where?' Mum said.

'We'd better go.' My laugh sounded ridiculous. 'I must have frightened . . .' My throat closed up. My eyes filled. I couldn't say his name – couldn't even say his name. I turned away, hid my face in Spicer's jacket.

He lifted my chin. 'We'll get some food, then go and get

him.' Those were the words that came out of his mouth. His eyes said something different. They told me he was as scared as I was. They told me he had a plan. They told me to trust him.

I sat in his car. We didn't speak until we'd waved goodbye to Mum and Dad and pulled out into the road.

'He isn't with your friend, is he?' I said.

'No.' His mouth was a tight line.

'And I'm not mad.'

'Not on this occasion, no.'

I wanted to be. I wanted his story to be true, even if it meant I was crazy.

'D'you know where they've taken him?'

'Oh, yes.' Tyres splashed on the tarmac. 'I know where he is all right.'

28. PEARL

We drove away, through roads I'd never travelled or at least roads I didn't recognise. A chill mist hovered over the fields on our right. All was quiet except for an occasional car going past. Other people with normal lives, with children perhaps, children who were safe. I wanted to be those people, live their lives instead of my own.

On our left ran a ramshackle stone wall, head-high. Beyond it stood trees and more trees, and they all looked exactly the same. I had no idea how long it had been since they took Lucas, or how far we'd driven. It seemed like hours. Perhaps it was.

'Can we call the police?' I said.

'No.'

I didn't ask why. He knew all about Mesmeris. He knew all about the police. After all, he was in both.

We turned into a road full of potholes, and bounced about, lurching from side to side. Huge gates came into view. Rusted, iron gates.

I felt woozy. 'I've been here before,' I said, although I couldn't think when, or why I'd have been there. Dread filled me, dragged me down, pressed me back against my seat.

'Déjà vu,' he said.

Yes. Yes, that would be it. Déjà vu. So why couldn't I catch my breath then? Why did this sickening dread make my head spin?

'I'm going to be sick.' I opened the door before he'd stopped the car and threw up over the mud and stones and grass. 'I've . . .' The world tilted, rolled. 'I can't . . .'

'All right.' He held me, his arms around my middle. 'It's all right, Pearl. It's all right.' He kissed the back of my head. I thought, he's crying, and I wondered why. How strange that he should cry. And it made me more frightened, because there had to be something to cry about, if he was doing it. He wasn't like me, blubbing all over the shop. He was a man. A proper, brave, wonderful man, and he only cried when there was something worth crying about.

'It's the car,' he said. 'The uneven road. It would make anyone queasy.'

I nodded, even though it wasn't that. We both knew it, but better to pretend and get on with things. Better by far.

He got out and pushed the gates open. I shut the door, leaned back, closed my eyes and tried not to remember Jack and Leo doing the same, so long ago.

Spicer climbed back into the car.

'I'm okay now,' I said. As long as I took deep breaths through my mouth, I was, as long as I didn't think.

'We'll park in the trees,' he said, after we'd driven a little way. 'Maybe we'll get in and out without being seen.'

He didn't sound too hopeful.

'We have God on our side,' I said, and Spicer snorted.

Still, I prayed I was right. I couldn't feel God watching us, helping us. I couldn't feel anything but evil, but I had to trust, didn't I? Had to have faith. That's what Dad always said – even when things seem hopeless. That's what he said, and I trusted my dad, didn't I? I believed in him, so I had to believe what he believed, even if it was hogwash, even if it was a load of old codswallop as Lydia called it.

The house didn't come as a surprise – the marble steps up to the old front door, the floor-to-ceiling leaded windows along the front of the house. They'd fixed the door, I noticed, so it wasn't hanging off its hinges any more. The windows too had been repaired. No ivy and brambles creeping through.

'I went mad here,' I said. 'In this house.'

Spicer stared.

'Jack left me here. There were sofas, two of them.' I pointed through the windows to where they'd been, all sagging and moth-eaten and smelly. 'And he left me.'

'I didn't know.'

'No, but Art did. Art was there. Art's here now, isn't he?'

'Yes,' he said, and then, 'I'm sorry, Pearl.'

'I'm over it.' And I was. I really felt that seeing the place again had laid the ghosts to rest once and for all.

'Stay here,' Spicer said.

'I'm coming with you.' I took a step but he pushed me back into the shadows.

'You,' he said, through gritted teeth, 'are going nowhere. *You*, for once in your life, are going to listen to me.'

I stared up at this new Spicer.

He released my arm. '*I'm* going in to get Lucas, okay? Now, if someone sees me, it may take me a while, understand?'

I nodded.

'Do *not* come in, no matter how long I take. If you do, you'll be risking your own life, *and* mine.'

'Okay.'

'And Lucas will never be free of them.'

'Right.'

'They'll know I brought you here. There'll be no escape for any of us. *Do* you understand?'

'Yes. Yes. I get it.'

A tentative smile. 'Do you trust me?' He had such honest eyes – warm, and kind and loving and true.

'With my life,' I said.

He kissed me, and vanished around the side of the house. And I thought how odd it was that I trusted him not only with my life, but with Lucas's too. I didn't, hadn't ever, trusted Art. Would I, when this was all over? I couldn't imagine it, not standing there, breathing in the evil. I couldn't imagine it ever being over, but I hoped. I hoped God would keep Spicer safe, because he was a good man. A really good man.

29. SPICER

Spicer strolled through the kitchen, up the steps and into the hallway, concentrating on his body language. He aimed for a relaxed saunter in case someone spotted him, even though his nerves were so tightly strung they hurt. Voices came from the study – Papa spouting off and sycophantic laughter. How he hated these creatures, these monsters. He headed for the stairs. The nursery was at the back of the house. He'd helped to set it up, painting the walls, hanging mobiles. It would take minutes to free Lucas. Easy. A doddle.

Ruby appeared out of her bedroom. 'Where've you been?'

'Where d'you think?' Sweat sprung out of every pore. 'Spraying blood in the house, like Papa told me.'

'All that time?' Eyebrows arched, she looked even more repulsive than usual.

'I got lost, okay?'

She sneered. 'You're such a tosser.'

The sound of the gong reverberated through the house.

'Dinner,' Ruby said. 'Better get down there.'

'I . . .' Spicer pointed at the bathroom. 'Just need to freshen up.'

She folded her arms, leaned back against the wall. 'I'll wait.'

Did she know? She couldn't. There was no way, but . . . He splashed his face with cold water, listened out for her going downstairs. She wasn't going anywhere. She was whistling Jerusalem. Hatred made Spicer's body go rigid.

He could kill her, get Lucas, get out of there. He hated her enough to do it. Yes, he thought. It was the only way.

She rolled her eyes as he came out of the bathroom. He avoided her gaze, ignored her snide jibes. He had to do this. She turned her back on him. Now. Now, he had to. Her neck was slender, breakable. The thought of it made him feel sick, but he had no choice. He raised his hands.

A click to his right and there was Leo. Shit. One of them, maybe, but not both. Spicer knew his limitations.

The three of them traipsed downstairs. Papa presided at the head of a long table. Black candles burned at intervals down the centre. Other candles flickered in sconces on the walls. Every surface in the room had at least one candle on it.

Skinhead filled everyone's glass, then sat at the end of the table nearest the door, almost hidden in the shadows.

'Tonight,' Papa said, 'we are complete. I have my heir.' He stood, so everyone else stood too.

Papa raised his glass. 'To Lucas.'

'To Lucas.' Everyone raised their own glasses and cheered.

Could Pearl hear them from outside? Maybe. Spicer just hoped she'd trust him enough to stay put. He made an effort to eat, forced down a chunk of roast duck, too bloody for his taste, liverish. Everyone else shovelled food into their mouths as if they'd been starved for a week. Malki's head was so low over his plate, all Spicer could see was the top of his head and the fork – plate to mouth, plate to mouth, like an animal. No, worse than an animal.

Leo rubbed his hands together. 'So I get to have my revenge at last.'

Papa turned to Ruby. 'The mother, she's . . ?'

'As you ordered.' Ruby sipped at her drink, but the glass didn't hide her sly smile.

They had it all worked out, and if Spicer failed, the world would believe their story. Pearl wouldn't stand a chance. Neither would Lucas. He'd turn out like his father, and Spicer wasn't about to let that happen. He couldn't fail, *mustn't* fail.

Malki raised his head. 'Won't she talk?' Then he flinched, as if anticipating a slap across the head.

Leo's expectant smile slipped. 'Talk?'

'They'll never listen to her wild stories.' Papa said, so smug, so sure of himself. 'She's unhinged, I'm afraid. Completely mad. It's very sad.'

Ruby nodded. 'Tragic really, wandering the countryside like a lost soul.'

'What?' Leo's voice rose – shrill, girlish, petulant.

Papa sighed. 'The poor child's already on the at-risk register. It is fortunate indeed that we were able to rescue him.' He chuckled, so Ruby did too, then Malki – hesitant, uncertain.

'You mean she's not here? The slag?' Leo glared at Ruby. 'You didn't bring her *back*?'

'I did as Papa asked.'

Leo shoved his face in front of hers. 'What about *this?*' He pointed at his eye patch. 'Papa said I could have her, do what I liked with her.' He pressed at his temples with clenched fists, eyes tight shut. 'I've planned it – all of it – what I'm going to . . .'

'I changed my mind.' Papa's calm voice chilled the air. 'Whatever sordid torture you had planned could never match the pain of losing her child, of knowing he's alive, knowing she's innocent and no one believing her.' Papa smiled. 'I have seen it before. She *will* go mad.'

Leo jumped to his feet, knocked his chair over with a clatter. 'Fuck that.' He slammed his glass onto the table. It shattered. Red wine spread over the white damask tablecloth. 'I'm having her now, and no one's going to stop me.'

'Leonard,' Papa growled. 'Sit. Down.'

'You said.' Leo pointed a shaking finger at him, as wine dripped from the table, staining the carpet beneath. '*You* said. *You* said I could.'

'Leonard.' Papa stood, his eyes bulging like a frog.

'No.' Leo shook his head. 'Fuck, no. No, I'm not having this.'

He kicked at his chair, kicked it again, smashed it against the wall. One of the fine, carved legs splintered and broke. Still he didn't stop, but roared as he stamped on what was left of the ancient chair.

It was like watching a car heading for the cliffs. Nothing anyone could do but watch Leo self-destruct.

Papa snapped his fingers and Malki stood, fists bunched at his sides.

Leo pulled a knife from his pocket. It flashed in the candlelight. A spasm of despair crossed his face as it crumpled.

'Go to your room, Leonard,' Papa said, wearily.

Leo's face contorted with frustrated rage and hatred. 'I am *not* a fucking child.'

Ruby chuckled, low and gravelly. Papa joined in, until everyone but Leo was sniggering.

Leo strutted towards the door, his body stiff like an automaton. Skinhead stuck his foot out and Leo tripped, almost fell in the dark.

Laughter filled the room as Leo stumbled out of the door.

Papa's face straightened first. 'I don't think we can let this behaviour go unpunished.'

'Can we watch, Papa?' Ruby gazed up at Papa with doe eyes.

Papa's slack lips stretched into an indulgent smile. One small nod, black eyes glittering.

Ruby clapped her hands. Spicer tried to copy the gleeful smiles of the others. He'd felt like that once, before the exorcism. He'd longed to see a murder. The prospect of it had been a turn-on, a thrill, a high. The memory sickened him. He was no better than them, after all.

Everyone stood and followed Papa from the room. Only Spicer lagged behind. He headed in the opposite direction, towards the nursery.

30. PEARL

Raindrops hit the top of my head – one or two at first, then more. They spattered the ground around my feet, growing heavier by the second. Something creaked behind me. I jumped into the shadows. The massive front door opened. Noises of a scuffle, groans, roars of anger and a man came crashing out, fell on his side. A figure emerged after him and slammed kicks into his stomach, his head. The noise was unbelievable – sickening thuds, groans and cracks. 'You're scum.' Papa's voice as I'd never heard it before – roaring, furious. 'You'll never be an Elite. Never.' Another vicious kick sent the lifeless body over the edge of the steps. He hit the ground with a soft thud. All was still, silent.

'Now,' Papa's face was clearly visible as he turned back to the house, the light illuminating his ugliness, the meanness of his mouth. 'It is time.' He went back into the house and the door closed behind him.

I inched over towards the steps and peered down. The man lay, broken, face down in the filthy leaves, in the drain. I watched for a moment in case he moved. I couldn't see if he was breathing. The leaves were wet. Would he drown like that, in the rain? Would he suffocate? I didn't know. For all I knew he was dead already.

I rocked back on my heels, rubbed my hands together, over and over, because I didn't know what to do with them. Whoever it was had to be something to do with them, with Mesmeris. To save one of them would be madness, wouldn't it? Madness.

I crouched down, and turned his head to free his airways. The eye was damaged, puckered, stitched.

Leo, my nemesis, my persecutor.

He wanted me dead, and yet I couldn't leave him, not like that. I heaved him onto his side and tried to arrange his limbs in some semblance of the recovery position. I felt his neck. The pulse was weak, slow, but he was alive.

A soft whisper came from nearby. 'Pearl.'

Spicer held Lucas in his arms. He had him, had my boy. He set off down the drive. I followed, running, running. Tears ran down my face. He'd done it – Spicer. He'd saved him, saved my child. Except we weren't safe yet and Spicer knew it. His long legs covered the ground as if the devil himself was behind him. Perhaps he was. I sweated and shivered at the same time. My scalp crawled, and still I ran, afraid to look behind. An icy shiver caught the back of my neck. The earth vibrated under my feet. Were they pounding after us? Papa? Leo? Demons?

By the time I reached the car, Spicer had already laid Lucas on the back seat. He lay there unmoving, lifeless. The woodland was as still as him, and as silent.

I climbed in beside him. He looked so pale. 'What's wrong with him?'

'Sedated,' Spicer said.

I cradled Lucas's head on my lap, stroked his hair. 'Sedated? Why?'

'They had plans for him.' We drove back down the drive, bumping and bouncing and still Lucas didn't stir. He weighed so heavy on my lap, like a dead thing.

'Will he be all right?'

'Yes.' Spicer smiled at me in the rear view mirror.

I had to believe him – had to.

'Did you see Art?'

Spicer's jaw tightened. 'No.'

'So he's not there?'

He shot me a quick glance over his shoulder. 'He's there somewhere. We went together, me and him, after your dad . . .' His mouth snapped shut.

'After my dad what?' My stomach knew before he spoke.

'Exorcised us.' The gates weren't open as we'd left them. They'd closed – not fully, but enough to make it impossible for the car to get through. 'Shit,' Spicer said. 'How the . . ?'

'Exorcised? He let my dad exorcise him?'

Spicer shook his head. 'Knew it,' he muttered. 'Knew you'd . . .'

'Why? Why did he let him?'

'Why d'you think?' He opened his door. 'Keep a look out.' Then he was out of the car and running over to the gates.

Art had gone through that horrendous ordeal for Lucas, to save him, and now? Now I was abandoning him, running away.

I slipped out from under Lucas, laying him flat on the seat, then I strapped him in as well as I could with two seatbelts and kissed his forehead. 'I love you. Don't forget.' Then I opened the door and climbed out.

Rain slashed at Spicer's face. His hair clung to his head like a helmet. 'Get back in.'

'They're going to kill him,' I shouted. A sudden gust of wind whipped my words away.

'You're insane,' Spicer yelled. 'He's as evil as Papa.' He

left the gates, ran back to me, and caught my arms. 'You have a child. Doesn't he mean anything to you?'

'Take him to my parents.'

'What about your family? Me? Aren't we enough for you?' His face looked haggard in the rain – and the hurt in his eyes. . .

I had to look away, stared at the ground instead.

'You have each other,' I said. 'Art has no one.'

He dropped his hands, stepped away. 'It's suicide.'

'Make sure Lucas is safe. Please.' Then I turned back to the house and broke into a run. The car door slammed behind me. The engine's roar grew fainter as he drove away, and I cried. I cried as I ran, but I had no choice. No one loved Art but me. No one else would try to save him. I was his only hope.

The drive was much longer than it had seemed in the car. It took ages before the house came into view. A strange recklessness took hold of me. I walked up to the front door. The brass doorknob was cold against my skin. I held my breath and turned it. One tiny squeak. Nothing really. The door made a sucking sound as it opened.

I remembered the hallway from before, when the water dripped through the roof into a puddle on the floor. I remembered the Victorian tiles, with their mosaic pictures of birds and flowers. The smell was the same too, the smell of the house, as if it was a living thing, although no longer mingled with mould and damp. Along the hallway facing me stood an open door on the right. A cupboard under the stairs perhaps. Light spilled out of it, and voices. I peered in, hoping the shadows would hide me. It was a cellar. The red-haired woman from nursery, the one with the killer heels, the one who'd brought Lucas out that day, the day of the scratch, sat on the bottom step. She was painting her nails with bright red nail polish. Two men, one with a shaved head, the other with oily muscles and greasy hair, scrubbed what looked like blood from the floor. Their laughter echoed, snide and nasty. The woman glanced up. I thought the darkness would hide me but she saw me all right because her smile faded as her eyes hardened.

She'd hurt my child, that bitch. She'd infected him, my innocent, lovely boy. My pulse hammered in my neck. I wanted to run, but my feet seemed glued to the floor. A thought occurred that perhaps these people *did* have powers after all. It took all my strength to lift one foot off the ground and to step back. It seemed to happen in slow motion, her realisation. Her mouth opened. I smiled. I think I smiled anyway, as my hand caught the door. 'Karma,' I said, and even the word was slow, drawn out. And I shut the door, shut them in there. Shut it and bolted it, top and bottom, trembling at what I'd done. I hoped no one would hear them in there. I hoped no one would ever hear them.

A thrill of adrenaline made me feel strong, powerful. I retraced my steps, turned right into the long room, the one that ran along the front of the building, the one with the floor-to-ceiling windows, the one where I'd lost my mind, that one. I walked across it, past the place where the sofas had been. There was new furniture now – leather armchairs, glass coffee table, standard lamps, even a pot plant whose fronds reached almost to the ceiling. It was still the same room though, and I knew where I was going, knew where Papa would be.

He'd be in the chapel, through the door at the end, the one with a sliver of light under it. I steadied myself, afraid my new-found confidence would make me careless, cause me to make mistakes. My mouth dried. My tongue stuck to the roof, and yet, despite my terror, there was elation too – crazy, unreasoning, illogical elation.

A cry of agony, muffled, came from inside. I pushed the door open. Papa had his back to me. The room was full of shadows and splashes of flickering, yellow light. Candles. Big, fat, squat black candles at intervals around the room just like before, held in the same sconces attached to the walls. So much the same, but I was a different person to the one I'd been then and that was Papa's fault – all his fault.

In front of that evil, heartless destroyer of souls stood a waist-high altar topped by a marble slab, and on top of the marble slab, lay a body. Art. Naked, on his back.

I must have gasped, because Papa's head spun round so fast it looked unnatural. His eyes were black holes in his face. His wet lips glistened.

'Ah, you're just in time,' he said.

Blood spattered the altar. Trickles ran down the sides, formed small pools on the floor.

'What are you doing?' A stupid question. It was obvious what he was doing. He was torturing Art, killing him slowly.

'He will be the sacrifice,' Papa said. 'And you will join him.' He lifted his face and on it was a look of absolute, sick ecstasy. 'It is perfect.' He breathed through his mouth as though breathless. 'Both parents. The blood of both spilled over my child.'

His child? His? My laugh sounded crazy, high and shrill.

'You have no imagination,' he said, with a snarl. 'You don't see it – the poetry, the symmetry.'

Art hadn't moved. He was the same colour as the marble altar top – as cold, as lifeless. An effigy of himself. Was he dead already? Had I risked everything for nothing? I didn't care that Papa was there. He didn't frighten me any more. He moved aside as I walked past him, his eyes watching me like a snake.

I took Art's chilled, pale hand in mine. 'You pulled his nails.'

'Did you know he ordered Jack's death?' Papa said.

As if I'd listen to his lies, believe a single rancid word that came out of his mouth.

'He was furious when I gave you to Jack.'

Gave me? As if I was his property? Art's bloodless fingers were ice cold. I clasped them between my hands and rubbed them, tried to bring them to life.

'And Jack refused to give you up,' Papa went on. 'Didn't you wonder why Art took you to that church? Took you to see Jack die?'

I was *not* going to look at him. I knew he wanted me to, wanted me to stare into his obscene eyes so he could make me believe him.

'Didn't you think it odd?' he said. 'Oh, no. I forget. You don't *think*, do you?' Each word held more venom than the one before. They came pumping out of his mouth, pop, pop, pop, one after the other. Snap, snap, snap, his lips went after each one, biting them off. 'You feel. That is all, no? Emotion – that is all that fills your *stupid* head. Do you have any idea how weak that makes you?'

He couldn't stand it, me refusing to look at him. It was

driving him mad, and that made me want to laugh, made me strong.

'You're a poisonous viper,' I said. 'You murdered Art's mother, his best friend, everyone who ever loved him, and now you're trying to turn me against him too.' I snorted. 'You're the weak one. You're pathetic.' Cuts, shallow slices, scored Art's skin at intervals. Blood smudged in patches, dark, and sticky – the only colour on his poor body. I stroked his hands, stroked his battered, beautiful face. 'He *loved* you, you stupid man,' I said. 'All his life he loved you and you do *this* to him.'

'This is nothing.' Papa's breath warmed my ear, moved my hair. He'd come closer without me seeing or hearing him. It made my skin creep. 'I've been – merciful with him. In *your* case, of course, I'll have no such compunction.'

A clattering sound behind us drew his attention. I ducked into the shadows, my heart stuttering.

A figure stood silhouetted in the doorway. Hair sticking up, dishevelled, spiky. And the smell – of damp and stagnant water. Leo. I caught my breath. Now I was afraid. Now I was so afraid that my body had no substance, was liquid, useless, so I couldn't have moved if I'd wanted to. He made a noise, Leo, something between a cry and a roar – pain, fury, despair all blended together. An animal sound. He hadn't seen me. He swayed back and forth, so I thought he would fall.

'*You.*' Papa spat. 'Get back in the gutter where you belong.'

'Papa.' Tears glistened on Leo's cheeks. 'Papa, please.'

'I *said*.' Papa took a step towards him.

Leo's hand held something. Papa saw it too, because he stopped. Silence, dead silence, and then a splintering crack, and another, and another – ear-shattering, one after the other, bang, bang, bang.

Papa's knees bent, and he knelt. Knelt in front of Leo. For a split second I thought this was it, the new order, then Papa fell forward. His face hit the tiles with a smack.

Leo dashed forward. 'No, Papa. No.' He knelt, lifted Papa into his arms and cradled his bloodied body. 'You can't die. You can't. Forgive me.' He stared at Papa's face, then flung his head back and howled.

Sobs, distraught, desperate sobs tore at Leo's body. His gun lay within my reach, but in a pool of light. I steadied myself. I'd need to be faster than him. It would take him a moment to realise, another to free himself from Papa's body. I could do it. I had to do it.

I inched forward.

My fingers touched the plastic of the gun, closed around it. I lifted it carefully, keeping my fingers well away from the trigger. Once I had it securely in my grasp, I shuffled back into the darkest shadows. The banging in my chest grew quieter as my breathing steadied. Leo was no threat to anyone any more, not hunched over like that, racked with grief.

His agonised sobs made me want to cry. He'd been a victim as much as anyone, just as much as Jack or Art. The ugliness of his face – the scarred eye socket – made me ashamed. I'd done that to him, and now, without Papa, he had nothing left. Maybe the violence could end now. I didn't hate him any more. I pitied him. I had the gun. I could offer him some comfort maybe. There was nothing to be afraid of any more. With Papa gone, the whole world would be different, better.

I was about to get to my feet, to say something to him, when Art's hand moved. So he *was* alive. Tears sprang into my eyes. It was all over. All over.

Leo straightened his back. His poor, ravaged face glimmered wet in the flickering light. How had I ever been afraid of him? Such a sad boy. He took the white inverted cross pendant from around Papa's neck and kissed it. Then he put it on over his head, and patted it against his chest. It seemed to console him. He smiled, and scrambled to his feet. Then he peered at the floor and paced about a bit, bent over. I realised he was looking for the gun. I drew back a little, my pulse racing despite everything I'd just told myself. He didn't come my way, but swore, put a hand into his pocket and drew out a knife – *the* knife, the one he'd used to kill Jack. He turned towards the altar.

'And now you, blue-eyed boy.' His icy voice sent a shiver through me. 'You wanna call me dickhead one more time?' He chuckled. 'I'm in charge now – not you, not Papa – me.' He moved towards Art, stood over him and the look on his face made me tremble. 'You like your eyes, don't you?' He grinned, raised the knife over Art's face. 'They're your power, aren't they? Yeah?' He leaned forward, tilted his head, his ear close to Art's mouth. 'What's that?' He stood, frowned, then put on a sad face. 'Aw! You want to keep those eyes? Yeah? You wanna keep them, but you know what? I'm going to take them.' He raised the knife.

I lifted the gun, held it with both hands. I couldn't miss, mustn't miss. I squeezed the trigger, my eyes shut. The sound reverberated around the tiny room. I forced my eyes open, afraid to look.

He wasn't there, Leo. No one stood there. He'd be coming for me, crouching down, that vile knife in his hand. I could almost see his twisted smile, smell his tobacco breath. I checked everywhere, behind me, everywhere. No sound. Perhaps I'd gone deaf. My ears rang from the gunshot. I thought my heart would give out as I crept forwards, crouched down low. I saw his hair, part of his head. I saw the mess, the spreading blood. His arm lay outstretched at an unnatural angle, unmoving, the knife balanced between thumb and forefinger.

I kicked the knife away out of his reach. I'd need it though, to cut the ropes. I bent down, picked it up. That knife. That knife killed Jack. That knife killed Abbi, I just knew it. If he moved, Leo, I'd use it on him. But he didn't move. I couldn't look at his face, what there was left of it, couldn't check his pulse. I walked around him and sawed at the ropes tying Art to the altar. He had his eyes closed. His face was deathly. He looked so much like Jack the last time I'd seen him, half-dead, bloodless. He's not Jack, I told myself. He's not going to die. This isn't the same – not the same at all.

'It's all right,' I said, and remembered I'd said it before, when it wasn't all right, when nothing was right at all, so I shut up and concentrated on the rope, on the knife cutting, cutting at the fibres. It was sharp, Leo's knife. It sliced through that thick cable as if it was nothing.

I didn't notice Art's eyes open, so when I saw him, staring up at me, I screamed.

His arms were free. He sat up and took the knife from

my hand without speaking. He was so thin, so bruised and cut, and I wondered if he'd ever heal, physically or any other way.

He swung his legs over the edge of the altar and winced as he dropped to the floor. I watched him, suddenly unsure of him, of anyone. He knelt next to Leo and put two fingers on the side of his neck. I had to turn away. Turning away made me see Papa. A small man, I realised. A weak man. A dead one.

Art stood and asked me something. My ears were still cloudy, so he had to repeat it.

'Where's the gun?'

'I don't know,' I said. 'I had it, but it's . . .' I waved a hand.

He pocketed Leo's knife. 'Never mind,' he said. 'It has your prints on it, but you won't be on their database.'

'I killed him.' For the first time, I realised what I'd done.

'Saved me a job.' Art smiled, put an arm around my shoulders. 'It's just you and me now, Pearl. You, me and our child.'

'Yes.' It was what I'd wanted for so long, but in that place, with the blood and the death, it felt all wrong.

'How did you get here?' He said it in a friendly way, but there was something – something not right, a tension in his voice, in the arm he held round me.

'Spicer brought me.'

'Ah.' He turned at a noise from the other room. 'Talk of the devil.'

Spicer rushed in, red-faced, windswept. 'Thank God.' He leaned against the wall, out of breath, as his eyes took in the carnage. 'Oh, thank God.'

'God had nothing to do with it,' Art said, an edge to his voice.

Spicer shook his head, closed his eyes. 'It's over.' He threw his head back and laughed as tears seeped through his lids. 'It's over.'

'Where's my child?' Art's voice clipped and hard.

Spicer's eyes flashed to me, back to Art. He looked as confused as I was. 'With Pearl's parents.'

'Right.' Art looked at me with a tight smile. 'Then we'll go and get him.'

'Yes,' I said, because that *was* the idea after all, wasn't it? That we'd be together? Me and Art and Lucas?

Art squeezed my shoulder. 'You go and wait in the car. I won't be long.'

'We're all going,' I said.

'Yes.' He blinked twice. 'Yes, we're all going, but Spicer and I need to clean up the evidence.'

'I can help.'

'You'll get in the way.' His jaw tightened. 'Wait in the car.' It wasn't a request. It was an order.

'It's okay, Pearl,' Spicer said. 'We won't be long. Just need to wipe a few things. Make it look . . .'

'As if we've never been here.' Art smiled – a wolf smile, triumphant.

I was halfway through the door when I realised I'd seen it, a flash of white on Art's chest. It was nothing, I told myself. A trick of the light. I went to the car – the one outside the front door, the flash, black limo. I pulled the front passenger door open, stared into the car. Something – something nagged at me. The white. I saw it again and I knew what it was. He'd taken it – Papa's cross. He'd taken it and was wearing it around his neck.

I went back, slow steps at first, telling myself I was wrong, remembering Art's tender kisses, his tears, his poor, battered body.

The cellar door, the one I'd locked and bolted, stood ajar. I froze, stared at the sliver of light. Had it been open when I came out? I didn't know, hadn't even looked that way. But they must have been freed, the girl with the red hair and the two men, and they'd be looking for me. I crept up the hallway and slowly, slowly peered around the door. The first thing I saw was a hand – a hand laying on the stone step – a hand with long, blood red painted nails. I watched it for a moment, the hand, but it didn't move, so I peered further round. She lay in a puddle of blood. Her hair was soaked with it. It had pooled on the stair, and dripped onto the stair below. On the floor of the cellar behind her lay the crumpled bodies of the two men. I shut the cellar door and bolted it again. I don't even know why. They were dead, that was obvious, but just in case. Just in case. I bolted it and ran towards the chapel, then slowed. I'd thought it was all over, just like Spicer did, but nothing felt safe. Whoever had killed the people in the cellar could be stalking us, could already have killed Art and Spicer. I crept through the long room. Dappled moonlight filtered through the tall, leaded windows. Shadows moved, flickered, made me catch my breath again and again. The trees. It was just the reflection of the trees. I crept and I prayed, prayed they would be all right.

No screaming, no yelling, no cries of pain, just voices. They were talking, Art and Spicer, chatting. I straightened up. When would I stop being afraid? Maybe never.

As I grew closer, the words became clear.

'You shouldn't have come back.' Art's voice.

No reply from Spicer.

I crept closer, slipped my hand into my pocket. My fingertips hit the smooth, hard casing of the gun. There it was all along. I hadn't lost it after all.

'You would only come between us.' Art didn't sound annoyed but chirpy, as if he was half-joking. 'And I can't have that.'

Still Spicer was silent.

'I reckon she'll give me a kid a year. What do you think? Ten years, ten kids.'

A child a year? A jolt of suspicion came and went in a moment. He'd been careful. He'd used protection. It was just a joke, that's all. He was baiting Spicer. Yes, that would be it – a joke, even though there was no laughter, least of all from me.

'My flesh, Spicer,' he said. 'All my flesh. I can build a new Mesmeris.'

My muscles froze. This was no joke. He wanted my boy after all, wanted to turn him into a monster, just like the monster *he* was. I forced one foot in front of the other until I could see them. Spicer was standing on a chair. His feet were at the level of Art's waist, his ankles tied together by rope. The same rope, the one I'd cut from Art. I looked up. His mouth was covered by black tape.

My heart stopped. I reached for the door to keep myself upright.

Spicer's eyes met mine. He looked away so quickly I thought perhaps he hadn't seen me, but he had. I knew he had, and he was protecting me, even then, even as Art was stringing him up he was trying to save me.

Art had a rope coiled in his hand. He scrambled up onto the altar and fed the end of it through a metal ring embedded in the ceiling. The other end of the rope was already tied into a noose.

My fingers wrapped around the handle of the gun. 'What are you doing?'

His head snapped around. I shrank back.

'I *told* you to wait in the car.' A nerve twitched in his jaw.

'Spicer's on our side, Art. He's not the enemy.'

'Get. In. That. *Car*.'

They say there's a fine line between love and hate. In that moment, I crossed it. A veil lifted from my eyes, from my brain, from my heart.

'Untie him,' I said.

Art's stare sent shards of glass through my veins. 'If you don't do what I say, *I* will have to get the child from your parents. And you don't want that, do you? Because you know not one of your precious, holy family will survive.'

He pulled the noose down over Spicer's head.

I couldn't let him do that. I couldn't. But the noose was already around Spicer's neck and there was no time. No time. I pulled the gun from my pocket and pointed it at the back of Art's head, at the patch of soft, vulnerable skin between his collar and his black hair. I held it with both hands. They were trembling so violently, I was afraid of hitting Spicer, but there was no point aiming for Art's leg. He'd have time to kick the chair away and then it would be too late. Too late.

'Art, please.'

He turned his head to look at me and his lip curled in a sneer. 'Don't be stupid. You won't use that.' Then he laughed – a mocking, vile laugh – just like Papa's. Just like it.

I took one last look into those beautiful blue eyes, and squeezed the trigger.

31. PEARL THREE MONTHS LATER

Spicer knew what to do, how to erase the evidence, and I helped him, wiping down anything we'd touched. He put the gun in Leo's hand and wrapped his fingers around it. Murder and suicide was the verdict. Leo had gone insane, killed the others before turning the gun on himself. One pathologist raised doubts about Leo's apparently self-inflicted wounds, but others disagreed and he went unheard. It was fairly obvious, after all, that they'd all killed each other. They were a cult, weren't they? A bunch of loonies, as the tabloids labelled them.

I expected to be traumatised, to be kept awake by nightmares, but no. I was absolutely fine. Papa had killed Art long before I shot him. He'd destroyed him from the inside, just like those parasitic wasps – eaten away at the real him until he was just a shell, a carapace – a beautiful, empty facade. Papa killed Art, not me. Papa killed Leo, Jack, and ultimately himself. There could only ever have been one ending for Mesmeris. And with their deaths it had gone, the evil or whatever it was that drove them, and the world felt safe again, light again.

Spicer took the cross from Art's neck. He took it and burned it until it was nothing but ash. Neither of us believed it held any power, but better safe than sorry, as Mum would say.

Lucas's exorcism was just as Dad had said it would be. Easy. A simple blessing. I'm not even sure Lucas noticed it happening, except for the sprinkling of holy water which made him laugh. There was no more talk of worms, just one very happy little boy who talked of nothing but having Spicer as his daddy.

We had the wedding in church – our old church. Mum cried. Lydia tried her best to look bored. Lucas beamed from morning until bedtime. I didn't wear white. It didn't seem appropriate somehow. I wore cream. Not a fluffy wedding dress, but a nice one nonetheless. Spicer wore navy blue. It bought out the honey colour of his eyes.

Spicer's mum came, with her carer. She sat in her wheelchair and kissed my cheek. She hugged Spicer.

'I think she knows,' he said afterwards, 'who I am.'

I nodded and hugged him. 'Of course she does.' Maybe she did. Maybe behind those vacant eyes, she remembered her son.

Why had I never realised how much I loved Spicer? Perhaps I'd been dazzled by Art's charm, blinded by Jack's horrible death, seduced by the excitement and danger of Mesmeris. Perhaps their power had affected me after all, just as it had Spicer.

His 'mark' was healing nicely, the doctor said. In time, it would be barely noticeable. I didn't hate it, the carving on his back. It was a sign of all we'd been through – a reminder of how lucky we were to have survived.

What I'd felt for Art wasn't love, hadn't ever been love. My counsellor had been right all along. It was infatuation, obsession, lust, all of those things, but most of all pity and a longing for him to be someone he wasn't, someone he would never be – someone good.

My bouquet was a bunch of daffodils. After the ceremony, I scattered them on the ground beneath the yew tree, where Jack was buried.

'It's all behind us now.' Spicer put an arm around my waist and patted my rounded belly. 'It's just me, you, Lucas and this little one.'

As if it had heard him, the baby kicked. A cloud covered the sun and a shadow passed behind Spicer's eyes.

A small doubt entered my mind. I brushed it away.

It was Spicer's baby.

Definitely.

ALSO BY K E COLES

MESMERIS

INFIXION

Printed in Poland
by Amazon Fulfillment
Poland Sp. z o.o., Wrocław